THE DARKEST LIGHT

ALSO BY VICKI-ANN BUSH

Alex McKenna & The Geranium Deaths

Alex McKenna & The Academy of Souls – Audible Edition

Alex McKenna & A Winter's Night - Audible Edition

UNTHREADED

Ophelia

The Garden of Two

Saving A Life

The Queen of IT

Winslow Willow the Woodland Fairy

Short Stories

The Joshua Tree

The Darkest Light

Vicki-Ann Bush

Published in the United States by Creative James Media.

www.creativejamesmedia.com

978-1-956183-44-3 (trade paperback)

First U.S. Edition 2024

This book is dedicated to my protector, my comforter, my friend . . . my mom.
Thank you, for never stopping believing in me and showing me the kind of love that built the life I have today. You were hot cocoa on a snowy day, chicken soup on a stormy night, a shoulder to cry on for my drama years, and my scary movie buddy.
I miss you so much, I'll love you forever.

ONE

Luke Jacobs reached over and slapped the snooze on his alarm. Rolling onto his side, he scrunched his pillow, propping his head up a few inches. A warm beam pierced the shell of the protective barrier between comfort and the desert's ninety degree fall weather. He sighed. A branch from the large velvet ash painted hues of deep orange and plated gold along the sill, adding to the illusion of a crisp autumn morning.

Throwing back his sheet, he slid out of bed. Running his fingers through his trimmed, chocolate locks, his gaze traveled to the royal blue and gold football jersey thrown over the game chair in the corner of his room. He smirked, visions of the winning score board were fresh in his mind.

He pulled the charging cord from his phone and scrolled through a few congratulatory texts for last night's game. *That's right, star quarterback in the house.* Three quick raps on his bedroom door dissolved the image of cheers from the stands.

"Yeah?" His deep voice still gravelly from the celebrations last night.

"Hey, are you going to the mall for Mom's birthday gift?"

He rolled his eyes before answering. "Why Becca, what do you want?"

"Can I come in? This is obnoxious."

Without waiting for a response his little sister barreled through the door.

"Hey, what the hell?"

"Sorry, but I need to talk to you." She quickly sat down on the edge of his bed. Twirling the ends of her golden mane, her green eyes focused on her brother. "Can I come with you? Dad was supposed to take me, but something came up with work."

He smirked, sat down on the chair at his desk, and swiveled around to face her. "I'm not staying all day. In and out."

Becca's eyes lit up and she fluttered a series of nearly silent claps. "I promise."

"Now leave. I gotta get dressed."

Becca padded across the room, a victorious grin on her face, and shut the door behind her.

Luke slid out the first drawer in his dresser and grabbed his black, Thrasher t-shirt. His jeans were on the floor by his nightstand and after a quick scan and sniff he decided they could go another day without washing. He'd showered the night before so a swipe of under arm deodorant was all he needed to be ready. Taking a quick glance in the mirror above his dresser, he raised a brow. His eyes were more red than baby blue. *Ugh, maybe stayed up a little too late.*

Plodding down the stairs he smiled, last night was worth the day after zombie look. The adrenaline still running through his veins from last night's win stole any appetite he'd normally have in the morning, but a cup of black gold was a must. Pulling down a large Yeti, he filled it to the rim and added a few drops of almond milk before pressing down the top.

"Becca," he shouted. "I'm leaving. Get your butt in the car."

"Coming!"

Becca slammed the passenger door shut and Luke glared.

The 2012, dark green Toyota Tacoma was an early graduation present from his parents. The buttery, caramel leather seats weren't ideal in the desert heat, but he loved the smell. The Tacoma had only one original owner and the guy treated the four-seater like his girlfriend. With an odometer just tipping 90,000 miles, the near decade old small truck was a sweet ride.

About halfway to the mall a loud screeching, like a bad violinist, pierced its way through the vents. His air conditioner was tired for the day. Luke cranked the window down and let his fingers brush along the small patches of patina on the driver's door. The parking lot was empty, looking more like Christmas day instead of a Saturday afternoon.

Luke pulled up to a spot only a few feet away from the main entrance; he gazed up to the glacier blue heavens where not one cloud neither obstructed nor enhanced the view. The mall in Henderson was nicer than some and less than others. But it was the closest to Boulder City and pretty much had every store he liked to shop in.

The black river of sand, gravel, and broken stones flowed to meet the banks of concrete waiting to usher in guests. Typically, the middle-class Joneses willing to part with their hard-earned cash for a shiny, new designer this or that. Luke had a plan though, so his budget and time would be limited in the house of couturiere.

"Hey, can we get a Cinnabon?" Becca gently shut her door.

"Uh, what happened to quick?"

"It'll just take a few minutes, and neither one of us ate anything before we left."

He hated to admit it, but his stomach had growled its way back to needing some sustenance and a sweet cinnamon roll sounded pretty tempting.

"Okay, let's go." Luke tapped the key fab and locked the doors.

Becca grinned. "I knew you couldn't resist a gooey bun."

"Whatever. Let's get in there."

He eyed the passing puffs of shoppers looking for a familiar face, but he didn't recognize anyone. Under a dome of white twinkles, the neutral tones of beige and cream tiles mapping their way to the variety of food stations caught Luke's attention. The gleaming store windows reflecting the fracture of light was reminiscent of their last family trip to Disneyland and Sleeping Beauty's castle. At night under the canopy of fairy lights, the allure flushed over him as if someone special shared their magic. It was a memory that stuck with him.

The counter at Cinnabon was empty and Luke chuckled watching three of the employees busily frosting pans of freshly baked yummies. He looked around the food court; you could kick a goal and not hit anyone. What were they gonna do with enough pastries to feed the entire population of his high school? One of the intense baking teens noticed him and came over. Several adjustments to the paper chef's hat propped up on his head was followed with glowing cheeks and a forced smile.

After their transaction was complete, the shy teen gleefully went back to frosting his pan of naked buns.

Luke set the food tray down and slid into the attached plastic chair. Swapping comfort for space, it felt more like grade school than a place to dine. Opting to saw the plastic knife into the steaming bun, he cut a small piece and forked it with another cheap utensil. He didn't realize how hungry he was until he took the first bite of sugary cinnamon. He was about to cut into another gooey chunk of goodness when without warning, his heart crushed against his rib cage.

Looking from side to side, a warning crawled along his veins. He stood up and surveyed the area, while an invisible force tightened around his neck like hands slowly squeezing the breath from his body. As he clawed to remove the pressure, his eyes bulged, and a curtain of darkness slowly took his vision.

"Luke! Luke! What's wrong?" Becca held a firm hold on his arm.

Like fingers slowly releasing their grip the tightness faded, and his chest heaved filling his lungs with air. Folding onto the chair he took a fluid drink of water, his throat relaxed, and he massaged his chest until his pounding heart slowed to a normal beat.

"Are you okay? What the heck was that?" Becca's eyes widened.

"I . . . I'm not sure."

Luke gazed past Becca and shivered. A stranger, about the same age as his dad, stared at him from across the food court. Luke shifted in his seat, a rising heat growing in his belly and then . . . her.

With a tray of pizza slices and drinks, she approached the stranger. Her plump, rosy lips pouted, suggesting she wasn't a willing participant in the festivities. A waterfall of dark tresses caressed the curves of her oval jawline and ivory skin. Her attention was on the man, who hadn't shifted his gaze from Luke.

Setting the tray down on a table, she pulled her hair back and twirled the unrestrained ponytail to a twist and knotted it. Dropping her shoulders, she turned to face the dining room and, for a brief moment, their eyes met. Luke nervously searched his body for a place to land his hands before slipping them into the front pockets of his jeans. His eyes rounded, his heart pumping, he should have looked away, but he couldn't. Her lips parted, turning the pout into a casual smile. He tingled with intrigue.

"Hey, you gonna finish that?" asked Becca.

"Uhm, what?"

"Your food?"

Luke glanced down at his plate, almost surprised to see it still there. "No. Lost my appetite."

"Okay, let's get Mom's gifts and get out of here. You don't look so good."

Luke's gaze traveled from the mystery girl to Becca, who had grabbed their tray and was dumping it into a nearby receptacle. Turning back, he wanted to soak in another look of the alluring beauty, but she was gone. He scoured the room for her—nothing. She and the man had both vanished.

Becca held her promise and picked up her intended gift in the time it took Luke to grab the new CD from Beth Hart, his mom's favorite. They were back on the road and headed for home in less than forty-five minutes. The baby blue had turned to an angry steel grey with ominous ribbons of black weaved into the afternoon sky.

"Damn, I hope it doesn't rain. Dad won't let us go tonight if it does." Becca frowned.

"Na, it's not gonna rain. It's the desert, grey skies yes, downpour . . . not so much." Luke flashed a toothy grin.

"I hope so."

After each win, the football team and friends would pick up fast food and go to the park to celebrate. This would be Becca's first time getting to tag along with Luke. She was a freshman and their parents agreed to let her go if Luke made sure she stayed in his sights.

He wasn't happy but he had no choice. Babysit, or stay home with the latest horror release streaming on a Saturday night while his teammates and friends chilled—not gonna happen.

A hint of pine permeated through the open window tickling Luke's nostrils. It was one of his favorite scents. Swiping his phone to Spotify, he tapped The Killers and set it on top of the dash. Jason, his best friend, and the fiercest left guard ever to play for Boulder City High, was meeting them at Taco Bell.

"I hope Karen's there; her mom was iffy about letting her go," Becca said, looking out the window.

"Jason's going, so I bet she'll be there too."

A river of onyx sparkled under the glow of a diming streetlamp as Luke pulled into the parking lot. The drive-thru was packed and he surveyed the area for an open space. Pulling to the back of the lot, he spotted Jason standing beside his tricked-out Subaru WRX. The 6'1 teen was easy to spot, his broad shoulders tested the stretch of his black, long-sleeve T-shirt, and his dirty blonde hair and hazel-brown eyes were the lust of half the senior girls at school.

Jason nodded at the truck. "Hey, get this, we're not the only ones here tonight."

Luke bounced out of his truck, his white Nike's catching a gleam from the nearby headlights. "Becca, don't leave the truck."

She rolled her eyes.

"What do you mean?" Luke crossed his arms and leaned against the bed.

"Damn Green Valley is here too."

"What the hell? Why? They got Taco Bell in Vegas." Luke clenched his jaw.

"Yeah, someone said they're pissed about losing last night. Said it was fixed.

Luke laughed. "Yeah, like we needed to fix it to win. They sucked."

"Well, I promised my dad no crap. I've got Becca with me."

"Me too. I'd be grounded for a decade if I get into a fight tonight."

"Let's just go in and get our food, forget those assholes." Luke ambled toward the door with Jason behind him.

The line at the register was no better than the drive-thru.

The guys chose to ignore the rowdy opposing team taking up half of the dining area.

Trying to tune out the obnoxious group, Luke spoke up. "Hey dude, I saw the most gorgeous girl today."

"Hot?" Jason bumped Luke's shoulder.

"Extremely. It was weird though. She was with this older guy, and she didn't look too happy."

"Did you talk to her?"

"Na. Didn't have time. She had really long, dark hair . . . it was spine tingling. Really got me. Oh, and her skin was like one of Becca's porcelain dolls. Perfection. I wish I could see her again. I have no clue who she is."

"Bro, does she look something like her?" Jason pointed toward the parking lot.

An icy puff tickled the back of his neck and he shivered, on the other side of the glass, the mystery girl and shifty mall guy walked toward them. "That's her."

Wiping his palms along the legs of his jeans, his foot slipped on a discarded wrapper on the floor. Sliding, his left leg splayed out in a near split as he grabbed onto the condiment counter. A soft grip on his arm steadied his balance and he looked up and into the creamiest light brown eyes he'd ever seen.

"You okay?" the mystery girl asked.

Luke's pulse raced. Two pools of honey blinked, waiting for an answer. A map of soft freckles scattered over her cheeks and across her nose. Dropping his gaze to the floor, he stuttered, "Yyyyeah. I'm . . ."

She offered her hand. Trembling, he reached out. Her skin felt like silk gliding across his flesh. Flashes of darkness and fire bombarded his mind, a spike of electricity snaked its way through his veins, jolting him back.

His mouth gaped as he struggled against the instinct to run and the burning in his chest to get closer. "What the hell?"

"Uhm, that was weird," remarked the beauty.

"Mary, what do you want to order?" asked the man.

"Mary? That's your name? I'm Luke."

"Hi." Mary put her hand on the man's shoulder. "Hang on Dad, one second."

"That's your dad?"

"Yup. Hey, mall guy, right? I saw you at the food court." A glow mapped across her pale cheeks.

"Uh, yeah. I took my little sister shopping."

"Cool."

"I haven't seen you at school. Are you new here?" *Please let her live here.*

"We moved into town on Wednesday. I don't really know anyone yet. This is my dad, Aaron," she said, gesturing to the man next to her.

The man glared, and Luke shifted on his feet.

"We can't stand here all night, what do you want to eat?" Aaron's impatience dripped from his words.

"I'll have two tacos." She smiled.

I can't believe I'm asking this. Luke's gaze dropped to his Nike's. "We're all headed to the park and uh . . . I wanted to know if you wanna come. You know, hang out and maybe meet some people."

Mary tugged on her dad's arm, and he peered over his shoulder, his glare focused on Luke.

"Dad, Luke wants to know if I can go with him and his friends to the park for a while. Would it be okay?"

"You're Gabriel's son, yes?" Aaron narrowed his eyes.

"Yeah. You know my dad?"

"Gabriel and I go way back. How many of you are going to the park? And how long will you be terrorizing the poor souls who live across the street from your victory haven?"

"Dad." Mary furrowed her brow.

"It's okay Mary. It's pretty much the whole team, their girlfriends, the cheerleaders and some of their friends."

"I expect her home by midnight, no later."

"Don't worry, I'll definitely have her home on time."

"Good. You don't want me angry with you." He gave Luke a twisted smile. His steel blue eyes dripped with ice, nothing like his daughters. Luke shivered. Instinct told him to be wary but the tingling in his gut didn't listen. He'd get to spend time with her, and that's all that mattered.

He held the door for her with his foot and they ambled to the truck, arms loaded with bags of Taco Bell's dollar menu. Mary politely tried to squeeze into the back jump seat, but Becca leaped out and let her get in front.

"Hello," said Becca, her voice dripping with curiosity.

Mary smiled. "I hope you don't mind me tagging along."

Becca met Mary's gaze and abruptly bent over. Squeezing her fingers into her temple's she seized with dry heaves before uttering a faint yelp. Mary abruptly turned away.

"Becca, what's wrong?" Luke peered at her from the rear-view mirror.

"I feel a little queasy, I just need to eat." Becca held her stomach.

Luke handed her a fountain drink. "Here, I got you a soda. Drink some, it might help."

He furrowed his brow, if he had to turn around to take Becca home he was gonna be pissed. He had limited time with Mary and he didn't want to waste it playing nurse to his little sister. He loved Becca, but sometimes she could be a pain in the ass.

He parked alongside the curb to the park. Pulling the key from the ignition, his nerves quaked firing off pings of excitement to his already eager brain. He stepped out from the truck, in the distant a quick flash of a serrated edge slashing through the starry black, stole a precious beat from his chest. Luke swallowed back the lump rising in his throat and slammed the door shut.

Becca widened her eyes.

"It got away from me, shut up." He shook his head. "You feel better?"

She nodded.

They carried their food to the picnic tables where Zeke was waiting, he was Becca's latest crush and the occasional object of Luke's torment.

"Uh, hi Zeke." Becca squeaked.

"Hi, I was wondering . . ."

Karen came running up and linked her arm with Becca's.

"Yay you're here, let's get our food and go sit over there." Becca motioned to a bench facing the playground.

"So, can I come too?" Zeke came up behind Becca, resting his chin on her shoulder.

Becca grinned. "Of course."

Luke and Mary walked to an empty bench on the other side of the playground. He scrunched his forehead trying to decide what to ask first. He didn't understand why, but he needed to know everything about her. The yearning clouded his mind, leaving little room for anything else. A pull from the center of his chest, inching him closer and closer would only be satisfied with answers.

Luke looked up at the denim sky, peeking from behind scattered balls of grey cotton. He shivered, a tingle at the base of his neck launched goosebumps mapping their way down his arms. He folded them close to his chest and briskly rubbed his forearms.

"Are you cold?" Mary asked.

"I'm starting to warm up. You didn't look too happy to be at the mall earlier."

"I'm not really into shopping. Honestly, I don't know much about fashion and my dad's not exactly GQ."

Luke chuckled. "Why'd you go?

"My dad thought it would be a good idea to get out of the house."

Mary's gaze followed the row of bungalows along the tree lined street. Once used for the men who helped construct the dam, they were part of the proud history of Boulder City, and now preserved as historical landmarks. The glow from the streetlight partially framed her face, highlighting flecks of gold of the honey-eyed beauty. Every muscle in Luke's body burned, urging him to reach for her. He pulled back, resting his elbows on his thighs.

Mary leaned in closer, closing the gap that separated them.

Luke sat up, accidentally brushing her shoulder. Visions flashed through his mind, a collage of Mary's life experiences, followed by a sudden stream of current that thrust him back and nearly knocked him to the ground. Mary jumped to her feet. She glared; pools of onyx replaced her warm honey eyes. She turned and ran.

Stunned, Luke ran after her.

"Mary. Wait."

"Leave me alone." she cried out.

"Please," he called. "Let's talk. I have no idea what that was. Your eyes . . ."

Mary halted and turned around. "You don't understand. It's better if you just stay away."

"You're right. I don't get it. So, tell me."

Luke caught up to her in the middle of the street. Small puffs of clouds followed their breath. His fists clenched to his side as a distraction not to say something stupid.

"Please, let's go back," said Luke. "I want to know. Whatever it is, you can tell me."

"This isn't any good. I thought things might be different in a new place, but it's not. It doesn't matter where I go, it will follow me because it's me—only me."

"I don't understand what you're talking about. Please come

with me, we'll talk." Luke reached out a hand and gazed pleadingly into her eyes. "I know we just met, and this is gonna sound weird, but I feel like I already know you."

After several seconds of silence, she gazed up at him and nodded.

"You wanna sit in the truck? It's kind of private."

"Yeah." Mary's smile didn't reach her eyes.

The short walk to the truck felt more like the buzzer going off at the end of a losing game. Emptiness had captured the butterflies in his belly, clipping their wings and leaving them to die.

Luke opened the door for her and started the engine to warm the cab.

Becca called out, "Hey, it's freezing, can you bring me the blanket from the backseat?"

He leaned on the door. "The truck should warm up in a minute, I'll be right back."

Mary blinked.

He hustled over to Becca and gave her the blanket. Karen scooted next to her, and two girls snuggled to get warm.

"Zeke," Luke said in a stern tone.

"Yeah, bro?"

"The blanket doesn't touch your skin. Got it?"

"I got it."

Becca rolled her eyes.

"I'm watching." Luke smirked and walked back to the truck.

As he approached the even hum of the running engine, Mary leaned over and popped the driver's side door open. Luke slid in, briskly rubbing his hands together.

"It's damn cold."

"Is your little sister having a good time?" Mary asked.

"Yeah, she is. This is her first after-game hangout," he chuckled.

"Listen, I know you want to know more about what

happened earlier, and I'll explain. But for now, could we just pretend this is a normal night?" She bit her lower lip.

Conflict gnawed at Luke's brain. *Yes*, he wanted to act like everything was normal, but caution whispered to his logic. He couldn't ignore what had happened . . . what he felt.

"Okay. Normal—for now."

Mary explained that her mom died soon after she was born. She and her dad had moved from Manhattan, and she hoped the move would be good for him. "It's more relaxed here. He's been uptight lately; I'm hoping he can chill out."

Her words buzzed around in his head, drowned out by the thumping in his chest.

"Luke, stop it."

"What am I doing?"

"You're staring at me."

"I'm sorry, you're so beautiful. It's hard to look away."

"You wouldn't say that if you really knew me."

"I'm trying . . ."

A shriek carried through the park and nestled on the back of his neck. A foul stench stung his nostrils, the air heavy with the offensive odor of sulfur.

He leaped from the truck, his rubber soles slamming into the pavement. Mary followed close behind him as they ran toward the girls.

The intruder stood well over six foot, a cumbersome frame with large muscles, and green glowing eyes. His protruding jawline accented razor-sharp teeth that rested on a thin, crepe, bottom lip. His dark hair matted to his head like a helmet, barely covering two deformities that one could only guess served as ears. He dangled Becca and Karen from their necks, one girl in each of his enormous fists. The girls sobbed, kicking their legs to wiggle from his grip, they dug their nails into the giant's flesh.

Zeke fumbled on the grass, bloody and staggering to get up.

One of the other guys ran to his side and dragged him out of harm's way. Luke advanced, the other boys close behind him.

"Stop right there, boy, or I'll snap both their necks like a chicken bone." The intruder's words resonated with a deep echo.

Mary stood behind Luke. He motioned for her to get back, but she wouldn't budge. He slowly pivoted his body to shield hers.

"Look, mister. We don't want any trouble with you. Just let the girls go and we can help you with whatever you need."

Jason inched up, standing shoulder to shoulder with Luke. "I'm with you bro," he whispered.

"Hah! You are as naïve as your father." The giant's deep voice possessed a haunting quality that raised every hair on Luke's body.

"My father?"

"Tell Gabriel that Abezethibou is here, and Astaroth is coming."

"Whatever you want, let them go." Luke's back stiffened.

"Better I show him."

The stranger slowly tightened his grip around Becca's throat. Luke watched in horror as the life drained from his sisters' eyes.

Both boys charged.

With a swift kick the stranger knocked them down like bowling pins. He kept a firm grip on Karen as Becca's limp body slipped to the ground. Dazed, Luke struggled to get to his feet, as another voice cried out. This one was different. Commanding , raucous. His jaw dropped when he realized where the dissonant voice came from.

Mary stepped directly in front of the stranger.

Luke yelled out for her to get to safety, but she didn't acknowledge him. Instead, she stood tall, immovable, like a centuries-old oak tree. He rushed to her side. Shock and terror swelled in him as he saw her face.

The pools of onyx had returned to her eyes, darkness filling the cavity where kindness once rested. They were twice the normal size.

Her soft, porcelain-like skin, now grey with crevasses mimicking the craters of the moon. Her once soft, plump lips were replaced with a cracked and blistering slit.

He struggled to draw in a breath. The frenetic beating of his heart deafened the sound around him.

Mary lifted her arms toward the sky and a bolt of lightning illuminated the atmosphere, sparking across the horizon it sizzled toward the park grounds. The stranger screeched in agony as the thunder stroke pierced his back. Crumbling to the ground his grip loosened, releasing Karen from his clutches. Jason scrambled to his sister's side, pulling her to safety.

Luke bent down to his little sister, cradling her in his arms as he shielded her with his body.

The stranger struggled to draw one leg under him, placing a heavy foot beneath his weight, he tested its strength before leaning to draw the other up, he grunted and pushed himself to his feet.

When he regained his stance, his gaze fell upon Mary. His eyes grew wide, and his mouth stiffened. He dropped one knee, bowing his head. "Mary . . . miss, I am so sorry. I had no idea you were here. Please tell Araqiel that I meant no harm to his daughter. I did not know he had arrived. I am acting directly on the orders of Astaroth, the Grand Duke. Please forgive me and take mercy."

Luke's thoughts spun around like a hurricane in his head. Mary's voice but not her voice, the piercing black pools that replaced her soft eyes and her words . . . *he wouldn't think she was beautiful if he knew her.* She frightened him and yet . . .

"Leave this place at once," she commanded.

"Yes, miss."

The stranger zipped down the empty space in front of him,

he took a step and vanished. A light breeze swept through the park bringing movement back to the night.

Terrified, the teens clamored over to the girls. Karen was breathing normally, but Becca was having a harder time coming around. Dropping her head back, with a thick tongue she murmured gibberish. Luke rocked back and forth begging her to open her eyes.

Mary approached and leaned over, placing her hand on Becca's chest. Becca's body quivered and she woke, her eyes clouded with confusion. Jason stepped in and pulled Becca from her brother's grip. Woozy, she leaned into his body for support. Luke scrambled to his feet and wrapped his arm around his sister's waist. Gingerly, he helped her walk to the truck as she swayed to retain balance. Placing her in the front seat, he secured her seatbelt. "You okay?"

"Yeah, just really tired." Becca dropped her chin.

Jason leaned up against the truck. "Hey bro, I'm gonna get my sister home but later, we need to talk."

"Yeah, I know. Is Karen okay?"

"Considering she was almost murdered—yeah, she's okay."

Luke nodded. He turned around and spotted Mary sitting at the base of a tall pine tree. His stomach roiled as he fought to swallow the acid painting the back of his throat. He swiped his sweaty palms on his pants and hesitantly ambled to her side. Standing against the tree he peered down, she met his look, tears trickling down her cheeks. Her eyes were once again the golden honey he'd had been drawn to earlier.

"What was that?" Luke gripped the steering wheel.

"I don't know. It just happens." Mary rubbed her temples.

"How did you know how to fix Becca?"

"When I was a kid, I saw a cat get hit by a car. I ran to it and . . . I don't know, it was like I just knew what to do. I jolted the cat back from near death, just like I did your sister."

"And that guy? Who is Astaroth and Abezethibou and what

do they have to do with your dad? And why did he call him Araqiel?

"I told you, Luke, I don't know. Maybe *he's* Abezethibou. I have no idea what he has to do with my dad. I've asked him why this happens to me, asked him to take me to a doctor or something, but all he says is there's nothing the doctor can do about it. He says eventually it will all make sense; I just have to be patient. But the older I get, the worse it gets. Whatever it is, it's killing me inside."

Her voice tugged at his heart. To see her in so much anguish was hard. He had no idea why someone he'd just met that day could have so much influence on his emotions, but she did. Truth was, he felt like he couldn't spend one day without her.

He reached for her, and she pulled away, looking into his eyes with a weighty sadness.

Mary leaned back, and Luke nervously put his hands in his jacket pockets. His brain told him to follow her lead—stupid brain.

"You're pretty cool for not totally freaking out tonight. The weirdness follows me wherever I go and usually people run."

Luke dropped his gaze to the ground and then slowly raised his head. Meeting her eyes he smiled. Sliding his hand from his pocket, he inched it closer to hers until they barely touched. Mary didn't pull back this time, with her index finger she traced the lines in his knuckle. Luke tightened his core hoping to quiet the flutters in his stomach. He traced the pain in her face with his eyes, the moon's kiss illuminated the dried tears on her cheeks. He was free falling into the unknown and had no intentions of pulling the cord.

He jolted when Becca rolled down the window and shouted her need to go home. He slipped his phone from his pocket and checked the time.

"Damn. I promised your dad you'd be home by midnight, it's fifteen minutes past."

They darted back to the truck and Luke hastily put it in drive, the shifter grinded.

"Auto abuse," said Becca groggily.

Mary lived near the historical side of Boulder City. When they pulled up, her dad was waiting with an open front door. He didn't look happy.

Luke walked Mary to her door. Her father's eyes were cold as steel, and his arms tightly crossed at the chest. The closer they got he focused on the bulging veins in the guy's neck—he readied himself for the confrontation.

Before he could say anything, however, Mary spoke.

"Dad, we need to talk. And don't try to blame Luke for my being late. Some creepy giant attacked us at the park. He almost killed Becca and Karen."

"What giant? What are you talking about?" His face softened almost instantly. "Are you okay? Did he harm you?"

"I'm fine. In fact, he knelt down in front of me and bowed his head. Told me to tell you he was sorry, and he didn't know Araqiel was here with his daughter. Why did he call you that? What did he mean?"

"Come in, and we'll discuss it."

"No. I want to talk about it now. Besides, Luke has a right to know after what he just went through."

"Luke, I'm sorry but I must ask you to leave so that I can speak with my daughter alone. If you have any questions about tonight, ask your father."

"How would my dad know about this? What's going on?"

Mary maneuvered herself in front of her father, standing inches from his face she tried to hold her ground. "Dad, you need to explain it to the both of us."

Aaron herded her into the open doorway. "Inside. We will discuss it there. Luke, good night."

Mary disappeared into the house, only to reemerge moments later.

"Mary—inside."

"I didn't say goodbye."

Mary leaned past her father, gave Luke a hug, and discretely palmed him a tiny piece of paper. "Call me later," she whispered.

"Wait, Mr. . . . I don't even know your last name."

"Malum." Aaron slammed the door shut.

Luke hesitated then walked to the truck, the vision of his little sister nearly dying by that thing in the park was too much to deal with and he struggled to hold back the tears. The night flashed through his mind like reels of film unveiling one horrifying moment after the next. Pulling into his driveway, he turned off the ignition and peered over his shoulder, Becca had fallen asleep. Her head pressed into the back of the seat, she'd drawn her knees to her chest, she looked so small. Running his fingers through his hair, he glared at the front door wondering what his dad could say that would explain the weirdness that had nearly stolen his sister. Whatever it was, one thing was clear—he was hiding something.

Two

Luke had a hard time taming his thoughts; nothing made sense. His fingers slipped and the driver's door slammed shut. Wincing, he checked around to see if anyone was outside. The last thing he needed was unwanted conversation from an over excited Boulder City High fan. He ran around the truck to help Becca. She was wobbly and could barely keep her eyes open. A twinge of guilt flooded over him; he should have never left her alone. Maybe he could get his sister to bed without his parents seeing her. If she had a solid night's sleep, she'd be better in the morning, and this wouldn't seem as bad when they explained it.

Propping Becca up against the house, he fumbled to get the key in to unlock the door. Click, he pushed the door open and wrapped his arm around his little sister. Becca gingerly followed his lead as they went inside.

Luke nearly lost his grip on her when he saw their parents, Gabriel and Cassie, standing in the middle of the living room. He'd wanted to confront his dad but after things were settled with his sister. Shifting from side to side to keep his balance, his muscles tightened with dread.

Rushing to Becca, Gabriel swept her into his arms. As he guided his daughter up the stairs, she murmured, "Mary saved me."

Luke folded into the cushions of the overstuffed, floral sofa. He knew Becca would be okay, she was just exhausted. Mary had warned him during the drive that it was a side effect of jolting her back. Tapping his foot on the tan carpet, he followed along with the song in his head . . . Bad Liar, by Imagine Dragons.

None of tonight made any sense—except for Mary. Luke lay his head back until he heard his dad come in and sit down. He quickly sat up, his dad's jaw had loosened, and his brows softened. The anger melted away.

"Who's Aaron Malum?" Luke clenched his fists.

"What happened to your sister?" Gabriel questioned.

"Who is he? For some reason he knows you very well. Told me to ask you about what happened tonight."

"When did you see him?"

"I'll tell you every detail about what happened tonight. But when I'm through, I expect the truth from you, Dad."

Gabriel nodded. "Okay."

Luke started from the beginning. When he mentioned meeting up with Mary and her dad at Taco Bell, his chest tightened. Gabriel leaned forward, resting his elbows on his knees, and clenching his hands. Brows knitted, mouth taut, he squeezed his fists tight.

Cassie quietly came into the room and sat next to her husband.

"That happens when you encounter someone like Mary and she uses her powers on you," said his dad. "You need to stay away from them."

Luke's mind reeled. "Someone like her? Powers? What is she? How the hell do you know all this?"

"I'm not sure you're ready to hear this. Not yet. In a few more months when you get a little stronger . . ."

"No. Now. You promised."

Luke's mom intervened. "Gabriel, we have to tell him. He needs to know everything."

"What do you mean?" Luke questioned.

"It's too much," His dad said shaking his head. His brows pulled together, and he let his gaze travel from his son to the pale green drapes framing the large picture window in the room. The new couch and light wood coffee table represented the results of his wife's month-long indecision. Gabriel sat up and placed a hand on Cassie's knee.

"What about his fulfillment, Gabriel? He's seventeen. In a few months he'll be ready even if he doesn't understand. You can't wait; nature won't."

Luke's dad sighed. "First, know that your mom and I love you very much. What I am about to tell you will sound unbelievable, maybe even ridiculous. But I assure you it's all true."

Luke cupped his hands over his face and slowly brought them down to his chin.

"You remember the stories from religion class? The ones about the archangels, the fallen angels, and God and Lucifer?"

Luke rolled his eyes; he wasn't looking for a religion lesson.

"Don't roll your eyes, I'm serious."

"Okay. What?"

"It's all true."

Luke's family were regular church goers, and he'd always imagined himself to be a faithful believer—until now. Disbelief burst from his chest in a short guffaw. "Angels?"

His dad's gaze settled heavily on him, and he nodded his head, scooting to the edge of the couch. "They're here. In our neighborhood. And I am . . ."

"And you're what?" Luke demanded, growing impatient.

"More time, we needed more time."

"Just tell me." Luke clenched his jaw.

"I am the archangel Gabriel. Your mother is the daughter of Priam, an immortal. We're here to protect the world, all of it, from the rise of Lucifer."

"What the hell are you saying? Is this your way of teaching me a lesson for Becca? Because believe me, I know I screwed up."

"The man you saw tonight is one of Lucifer's disciples, Abezethibou. He's true evil, an archdemon."

Luke cocked his head to the side, his brows tightly knitted below the creases folding on his forehead.

"Yeah okay, you don't want to tell me the truth. Whatever. What about Mary?" Luke's voice cracked.

"Her father's real name is Araqiel. He's a fallen angel who sided with Lucifer in the war against the creator and was banished to Hell.

"Over the past forty years, they've systematically been escaping from the underworld. Eighteen years ago, Araqiel subdued a mortal woman, who gave birth to a daughter. He killed the woman and named the child Mary—a mockery to God. What better insult than to name the evil spawn after the beloved mother of His son?"

"She isn't evil. She saved Becca. If she weren't there, we'd all be dead. That thing wanted to send you a message. She saved us."

Gabriel raised his clasped hands to his chin. "But one day soon she will reach what we refer to as fulfillment, and the Mary you know will be gone. She will be her father's daughter—a servant of Lucifer."

"Say I believe this crap you're telling me, if she's half human, she could fight it. I'll help her, I know she's good."

How did everything get so screwed up? He saw a girl he thought was hot, it's not supposed to be the end of the world. He stood up and paced across the room. Pulling his T-shirt away from his neck, he blew a gust of breath down the collar to cool off his chest. His pulse throbbing in his temples, he rubbed them to quiet the pain.

"Come on dad, what's the truth? Are you like in witness protection or something?"

"Son. Did you hear me?"

His gaze crossed from his mom to his dad. The man's lips were moving but Luke's ears were deaf from the pounding in his chest.

"You just met the girl," said Gabriel. "You cannot know anything about her."

"Well, I do".

"Impossible. She is Araqiel's daughter, you are the son of an archangel."

"She can beat it."

His mother spoke gently. "I can see you think you have feelings for her, but you haven't had time to let that grow. You met Mary hours ago and now you're willing to be reckless because of that? True emotions need time to nourish, blossom. What you're feeling is an attraction."

"No mom, you don't get it. First time I saw her my soul yearned, reached for her. Whatever—we're drawn to each other. I'm not letting go."

She stood up. "Gabriel, show him."

Luke's dad sat back on the couch and cocked his head to look at his wife, her intense glare was all the incentive he needed.

Pressing his fists into the seat cushion, he used them as leverage to force himself up. Navigating to the center of the room he took his shirt off and bowed his head for a moment. Then, raising his arms up to the heavens, he released from his back a seven-foot spread of white and grey wings.

Luke gasped as he pressed himself deeper into the corner of the couch, crushing the cushion with a steel grip. It was still his dad . . . right? Eyeing the feathery anomaly protruding from Gabriel's back, he dropped the cushion to the floor and slowly rose from the couch. Cautiously he mustered up the courage to walk to his dad. Reaching at first and then pulling back, he gulped. Closing his fists and opening quickly, he reached again. His hand shaking, he glided it along the wispy outline. They were strong, muscular, pulsing with life under Luke's hand, the feathers a soft down with a firm spine. Gabriel batted them slightly and Luke stumbled.

"It's okay. It's still me."

"Is this real? Because they feel pretty fucking real."

"Luke. Language," his mom hissed

"Sorry."

Gabriel smiled, then folded his wings, absorbing them into his body.

"We'll need to call Peter and Martin," Gabriel said, glancing at his wife.

"Why would you call them?" asked Luke.

Gabriel sighed. "Peter is an apostle and Martin is an angel."

"Wait, so when you say apostle, you mean *the apostle*?"

"Yes. I know this is overwhelming."

"Well then imagine how Mary feels. I'm going to her."

"I won't stop you, but you can't go alone. Araqiel will be arming himself."

"Gabriel, how can you take him over there?" Cassie asked. "It's too risky"

Everything about this evening cluttered Luke's head. He didn't want to admit to the paralyzing fear overtaking him. If Araquiel was an archdemon and Mary was even stronger, that meant that her father possessed serious powers. The mere mention made his stomach twist in knots.

Catholic school and church had made him completely aware of the potential of absolute evil. How could this now be a reality?

"What were you talking about when you said I was like you?" Luke asked. "I'm an archangel? Is Mom human, even if she is immortal?" The words pierced his brain like an ice pick . . . immortal. "Right?"

Cassie smiled at him. "I am human. Becca is human, but you will be as your father is. You are destined to be a soldier, a defender of the light. God made it so. When we were granted our lives together, your dad and I knew there would be a price to our love."

"You and dad sold me out?"

"What? Never." Cassie's eyes widened.

"You basically said that you guys were in love and in order to be together, you offered your first born," Luke said angrily.

"Pledging your love to the Creator, defending Heaven, and standing by the original seven is the greatest honor for an angel"

"The original seven?"

"Archangels. Michael, Gabriel, Uriel, Chamuel, Jophiel, Raguel, and Raphael. These are your brothers Luke, your family. You will be called on to aid in the war between Heaven and Hell. Lucifer can't be allowed to accomplish his goals. Everything you know, what every human knows, will be destroyed if that were to happen."

"What about Jason? Is he an archangel too?"

"Jason is an angel, not archangel.

"Is everyone in this town divine?" screeched Luke.

"No. Just those of us who live on Ramona Lane."

"What's next?"

"Astaroth. He is the grand duke of Hell. Lucifer is sending him to begin war on earth. He is no longer content with being prince of the underworld. After his defeat, when he tried to take Heaven and God banished him, he was satisfied with corrupting human souls to gain new residents in Hell. But Lucifer has become tired of his banishment, once again rising up to rage war against God and Heaven." Cassie grabbed her husband's hand and kissed it.

"Michael defeated him before, but he has been growing

more powerful," she went on. "The seven will need help. That is why our union was sanctioned by God. He knew if the human race was going to be at risk again, his army must understand what and who they were truly fighting for. An angel who is half human possesses compassion an archangel cannot. He feels what we as humans feel. He knows what it will take to lead an army that believes in their cause completely."

"I don't get you. Why wait to tell us?" Luke paced.

"We wanted you and your sister to have a normal life for as long as you could. We knew what this would do to you. We chose to wait. To let you be human, if only for a short time," Cassie soothed.

"And Dad? How has he . . . how has everyone blended all this time?"

"It's helped to have the angels live among humans to adapt. Lucifer is bitter, he wants revenge for an eternity in hell. If the angels understood how humans think, it would make it easier to figure out the devil's disciples and hopefully help to defeat him from breaking free from the underworld.

Luke squatted on the edge of the sofa. A sharp pain hammered in his head, drilling behind his eyes. His lids weighted and he closed his eyes, burying his head in his hands. His mom and dad sat down beside him, each leaning in creating a Luke sandwich.

This was who he was now.

Everything he had thought about his future had changed in one night. But at least he wasn't alone, Jason and the others would be learning the truth.

In the meantime, he needed to get to Mary. If her father influenced her to Lucifer's side, he could lose her. He had faith he could bring her to the light. It had guided him for seventeen years, why stop now. They would defeat Lucifer together.

"I gotta go to her now." Luke stood up, but Gabriel grabbed his arm, pulling him back.

"Araqiel is not going to just let his daughter go. She possesses enormous power from what you've told me. She's an important part of his plan. I'm sure of it." Gabriel walked to the hall closet, tapped the inside of the door, and it opened.

He waved Luke over. On the other side of a seemingly solid piece of wood was a room. He ran his hand along the front of the door and tight fisted, gave it several knocks. Following his dad's lead, they stepped through the frame and into a space about the size of his bedroom.

The walls were lined with a smorgasbord of weapons, some Luke recognized and others he had never seen before. Gabriel lifted a dagger off the wall, which he handed to Luke, then proceeded to grab a bow and arrow for himself.

"That's enough for now," Gabriel stated.

Outside the room, Gabriel tapped the door again and the room disappeared.

"This dagger was once used to banish Astaroth to Hell. It's blessed by Jesus, and, if used by the right hands, will protect the warrior who is wielding it. Luke, I wanted to shield you from this responsibility as long as I could. I know it's overwhelming. But you're strong, and I should have considered that. For tonight, only use that dagger if you absolutely have to. Tomorrow your training will begin.

"I'll help you get Mary," Gabriel continued. "But understand what I'm telling you. If she has a light in her, as you say, then she will come with us willingly. But be prepared, she may choose the darkness."

"She won't. I feel it."

Luke took the wheel so his dad could make a few calls. Gathering the cluster of angels that resided on Ramona Lane was surprisingly easy. Their fellow brothers required little explanation, just direction from his dad.

Stopped at one of the few lights in Boulder City, Luke listened to the one-sided conversation as his dad delivered the order that the two older angels would follow. Take the human grandchildren into hiding; they needed to be protected. The words swam around in his head roiling a wave of dizziness. *Get a grip Luke. You'll be useless to Mary if you can't shake this.* The light turned green and Luke white knuckled the wheel and took a few deep breaths to slow the thundering in his chest. He adjusted his shoulders as trickles of water cascaded down his back. Swiping the back of his neck with the palm of his hand, he wiped the moisture onto the thigh of his jeans.

When they pulled up in front of Mary's house, the lights were off. Luke's phone pinged, stealing a breath from his tight chest.

"Hey J, I can't ..."

"Bro, I know you talked with your dad, do you believe this? I'm losing it here. My dad, your dad . . . the devil. That stuff at the park was weird but this . . . I'm freaking out."

"I know, and we'll talk in the morning, right now I gotta go." Luke could still hear Jason rambling as he hung up.

Gabriel grabbed the bow and tucked it behind his back before marching onto the porch and knocking on the front door. Luke crept around back, trying to locate Mary's bedroom window.

A spine-tingling scream drilled into Gabriel's ears, and he looked up. Araqiel had snatched Luke and was circling twenty feet above the house. Gabriel released his wings and took flight.

As he ascended, Mary ran out the front door, her eyes widened in horror.

"So, Gabriel, here we are once again," Araqiel snarled. "This time will be different, though. Keep your distance or I will drop him. He is, after all, half-human. He has not reached fulfillment.

His little human body will lose its battle with the concrete below. Poor broken Luke will not be able to be put back together. And you, Gabriel, will have failed our Father. Oh, poor, poor Gabriel. What shall we do about this little dilemma?"

"Give me my son, Araqiel, and I will let you live for today," Gabriel commanded.

"Ha! I don't think you fully appreciate the situation. I am in control of your son's life right now, not you."

Gabriel's gaze locked on Luke, his face taut with fear. "Luke. Luke, look at me. You're going to be okay. Everything is going to be fine."

"You are such a fool. Always dabbling in your art of persuasion or is it communication?" said Araqiel scornfully. "Well, communicate this: Luke, you are about to die. Watch, Gabriel, as your son plummets to the ground." Smirking, Araqiel released his grip.

With sharp precision, Gabriel whipped out his bow and sent an arrow into Araqiel's left shoulder. The archdemon wailed and plummeted to the river of asphalt below. Gabriel swooped beneath his son and caught him just before he hit the concrete.

Mary screamed, running to her injured father. "How could you do such a horrible thing? Luke never hurt you or me. Why?"

"Mary, go inside."

"No." Her eyes were wide with darkness.

"You will obey me," Araqiel ordered.

"You've been lying to me all my life. I knew I was different. Now I know you've been hiding things from me. Why couldn't you just tell me?"

"I said go in the house. We will not speak about this here." Araqiel snarled.

Mary clenched her fist, her face taking on a sinister tightness. "All those years . . . I thought I was going insane."

Luke struggled to his feet, rushed to her, and grabbed her hand in his.

"Come with us. Please. Your father serves Lucifer."

"I know. I know who I am, who he is, and who you are. He told me everything." Tears streamed down her cheeks, she quickly wiped them away and stepped back.

"We can talk about all of this but now we need to go," Luke said, tugging her hand.

She didn't move. "He's hurt." Her face softened.

"You see, boy, she is my daughter of darkness," said Araqiel faintly. "Mary, come help me into the house. We have much to do to prepare. Astaroth is coming."

Mary looked to the stars, then into Luke's eyes.

"I'm not, Dad," she said.

"You are not what?"

"I'm not all darkness. I don't want to prepare for Astaroth, and I don't want to help you hurt anyone. I love you Dad, but I can't be like you."

Araqiel's face twisted in rage, his eyes darted from Mary to Gabriel. Sneering, the words dripped from his tongue like poison. "Go. But your true nature will come out on your eighteenth birthday. You will not have a choice. You are from me, and like me you shall be."

"But I'm also from my mother. And she didn't die in childbirth, did she? You killed her." Mary's voice deepened as her body stiffened.

"Sacrifices have to be made."

"Sacrifices? She was my mother."

"Enough! If you go with them, I won't be able to protect you from Astaroth. He is coming. If you betray him, you will feel his full wrath. If you are with them, *defending* them, Abezethibou and Abaddon will no longer bow to you. They will try to destroy you."

"Let them come." Mary turned to face Luke's dad. "Mr. Jacobs, if you'll let me, I'd like to help you."

Gabriel nodded.

As he watched his daughter walk away from him, from all the plans he'd made, Araqiel pulled himself up and went into the house. In the front room stood a cabinet made from five-thousand-year-old Abarkuh Cypress, one of the oldest trees in existence. He unlocked the doors, revealing a small altar. In the center was a statue of Lucifer sitting on a throne of bones, a nest of snakes at his feet. Several small figurines represented his worshippers, kneeling before the prince of darkness. Araqiel picked up two of the larger figures. Closing his eyes, he chanted an ominous prayer to his dark lord. The house rumbled with the magnitude of a six-point earthquake, followed by a sinister boom.

Standing before him bowed Abezethibou and Abaddon.

THREE

Luke's gut thrashed like crashing waves at Santa Monica beach—the southern California beauty where his family vacationed last summer. The chatter from inside his home on Ramona Lane grated on his ears like metal under his dad's electric grinder. Everyone Gabriel had reached out to were now guests in his parents' house and he wasn't in the mood for crowds. Exchanging glances with Mary, he suspected she felt the same . Her slumped shoulders reminded him of Benjamin. A quiet kid in school who sat in the back of the class. His rounded shoulders and tendrils of hair dangling in front of his face made the guy nearly invisible.

Twinkles nestled deep in the midnight blue sky rained down on the crushed granite walkway, illuminating the path to the front door. Gabriel walked ahead, ushering them into the threshold of a new world. One that Luke would like to forget.

With Mary by his side, Luke's eyes widened at the faces he'd known most of life. Friends of his parents he'd shared holidays with, all gathered in the living room—all in a defensive stance with their eyes focused on Mary.

"Stand down brothers and sisters. Mary came of her own

free will. Araqiel has proven to be as demonic as he has been in the past. His daughter chose the light."

Peter, his dad's best friend, interjected, "Choosing the light today doesn't mean she's on our side. We all know her fate."

"Not her fate, her choice. We can help her, and she can help us."

Luke spoke up. "You're judging her before you even know her. I've known you and I trusted you." He shot a glare at Peter. "You lied to me. You're angels for Christ's sake. Sorry dad. You're supposed to be all holy and I get you thought you were protecting your kids, but your lie nearly cost us our lives tonight. Mary saved us, not you."

"I understand you want to have faith in Mary, but history tells a different story." Peter scowled.

"Enough." Gabriel raised his hand to stop. "Mary's staying. Michael is aware of the situation, and he agrees with me."

Mary leaned into Luke and whispered in his ear, "Michael?"

"Yeah, he's kind of the angel big wig."

"Do you mean the archangel Michael from all the paintings in France?"

Luke chuckled. "That's one way to describe him."

Mary crossed her arms. "My dad didn't say anything about him."

"He probably just wanted to tell you about his annoying AF prince of the rejects."

"I'm thinking you mean Lucifer."

"Yup."

"Well, that's one way of putting it." She smirked.

Gabriel clapped his hands together. "We have a lot of work to do. Michael will be here within hours and the kids need to start training toward their fulfillment. That's all for now. I wanted you to meet Mary, there's trays of food in the kitchen, and you all know your way around our house. I think it's best we stay together tonight, and we'll commence in the morning."

"I need some air, you?" asked Luke.

Mary nodded.

He held out his hand and she loosely took it. They walked through the kitchen and out the sliding glass doors into the backyard. Two half-moon-shaped stone benches were placed on either side of a circular fire pit that brimmed with azure glass stones in the far corner. The chuckwagon style steel, black BBQ sat on the outer edge of the stucco patio facing four oversized, rattan chairs with cushiony aqua pillows, strategically placed to engage in conversation with the cook. Three round picnic tables and an assortment of chairs were scattered around a free-form in-ground pool, completing the picture-perfect backyard for middle America.

He sat down and surveyed the space. The archangel Gabriel owned a barbecue. A nervous laugh did little to lighten the mood. Moving his thumbs along his fingers, he nervously cracked each knuckle one by one, until he rested his hands in the pockets of his hoodie.

His gaze shifted to Mary. He couldn't stop the pull that captured him and yet, who was she really? His head and his heart were at war. The only thing he was sure of was his desire to be with her. The constant barrage of firing nerve endings every time he got close didn't repel him, but rather left him wanting more.

Mary sat down on a rattan loveseat near the pool. "For the longest time I was afraid to know who I was." The corner of her lip quirked, but the almost smile didn't reach her eyes. "All those years, I thought I had some kind of rare disease. That my father knew but was trying to shield me from, keep me safe from the truth somehow. I was so stupid."

"No, you weren't. You're like any other kid, you believe what your parents tell you because well, they're your parents."

"Sure, but who do you know has a disease that makes their eyes go black and can move crap with their minds? Or cause someone to have an electric jolt? No. I wanted to be blind. I chose to be in the darkness."

"I think you're kind of forgetting something."

"Oh yeah, what's that?"

"Demon dad."

Mary gazed up at the billowy travelers gliding across the darkling day.

"I'm sorry about your dad, and your mom too. I wish there were something my dad could do to change him."

"That's impossible. My dad is the darkness and yours is the light. There's nothing he can do. It is what it is." She paused. "I feel so betrayed by him. My mother must have suffered so much. She was an innocent soul; she had no defense against his evil."

Mary ran her fingers over the plush cushions.

"I wish I had known her," she said wistfully. "Do you know I've never even seen what she looked like? He didn't keep one picture of her, not one. What if he's right? What if I don't have a choice? I'm so scared of what I am capable of. If I ever hurt anyone, I could never bear it. I could never ..."

"Stop. You won't hurt me, or anyone else. Anyone good, anyway. I'm pretty sure knocking an archdemon on his ass is acceptable." Luke shoulder bumped her, and they exchanged a smile.

"I believe in you. Hell won't know what hit it." He bared his teeth and roared.

Mary chuckled.

"It's nice to hear you laugh," he said.

Gabriel peeked out from the glass doors. "Son, we need you both inside."

Traipsing into the living room, Luke scanned the packed area. The adults had gathered again but this time with the addition of their children. Jason and Zeke ambled to his side and Becca and Karen sat on the floor by the fireplace. Luke's gaze softened; the corners of his mouth drooped with sadness.

Yesterday his little sister's biggest worry had been ninth grade. Now her whole world had changed. All of theirs had.

Gabriel took a place in the center of the room and the low hum of voices silenced.

"I know this is difficult for all of you to comprehend but we don't have much time," he said. "Your parents have explained where we stand and what needs to be done, but let me review, and then I'll answer questions."

He gestured for Cassie to join him.

"No matter what was said earlier, Mary's our friend," he continued. "If Luke believes she will choose light, then I trust him. She proved herself last night and we can use all the help we can get. We defeated the army of Lucifer once before and we will do it again.

"All the mortal children have been taken to safety. I know this is difficult, but your siblings were at risk staying here. Only Michael knows their location. When this war is won, we will retrieve them.

"There are some things that need to be clear. All of you here are angels. Whether half-angel, angel, or archangel, you're all brothers and sisters against the darkness."

Luke spoke up. "Becca is human. Why isn't she with the others?"

Cassie grabbed Luke's hand. "Becca is human, yes, but immortal like me. She'll fight with us."

Luke locked his teeth and slammed his fist into the back of the recliner. What kind of screwed-up cruelty was this? Becca should be with the others—she should be safe.

"She's human, let her be human. What difference will it make?"

A voice rang out behind him. "She will turn the tide of the war."

Every adult in the room suddenly rose to their feet. Luke turned to see who could inspire such attention.

Towering in the doorway, a man nearly six and a half feet tall. Strikingly handsome, his chiseled chin and strong jawline highlighted the curves of his prominent cheekbones. His honey pecan strands captivated the eye as endless waves caressed his shoulders. Luke blinked, taking a second look, he realized the man's eyes were the color of violets.

Gabriel immediately embraced him. "Michael."

"Good to see you brother, all of you."

Michael meandered toward Becca. She stepped back, peering up at the mysterious giant who towered over her. Biting down on her lower lip, a drop of scarlet salt stained the back of her hand as she wiped it away.

Michel held her gaze. "To answer Luke's question, you will be critical to winning this war. You have the emotions of a human but the diligence and strength of an immortal. You are a pivotal component to our strategy." Michael bowed his head to her. "You child, possess the gift of sight."

Becca whipped her head around to face her parents before Michael's deep voice brought her back to face him.

"I'm told by your father, that you felt an extreme pain when you first encountered Mary. That is your sight warning you. It will work like a light that shines on anything or anyone that reflects the darkness. Eventually, in time, you will learn to use that power correctly."

Luke hesitated, shifting his weight from left to right. Michael's proud stance and taut physique shook his insides, but he'd always been a protective big brother.

"Becca was given a few extra minutes of being a kid as a reward so she could battle the prince of darkness?" his voice trembled. "I don't understand, if she's like mom then doesn't mom have the gift of sight too?"

"Luke." Gabriel motioned for his son to sit down.

"No, Gabriel, it's okay. He's feisty. Reminds me a bit of

someone else I know." Michael walked directly to Cassie. "Hello, beautiful." He leaned in and kissed her cheek.

"Hello, Michael. Good to see some things never change. You're still mesmerizing the girls." The adults laughed.

"Becca is a necessary asset," said Michael, turning to Luke. "Yes, she is like Cassie, but your mother no longer possesses the gift of sight. An archdemon stole her power. I promise you we will do everything to protect her and the rest of the children. We will fight to save them and all humanity."

"Which brings me to training. Every one of the children here needs to begin today. We no longer have the luxury of time. Lucifer is sending Astaroth far sooner than we anticipated, so we need to prepare."

Michael gestured toward Mary. "Come here, child."

Mary stood up and, shaking uncontrollably, wobbled over to him. His strength and command filled the room with an almost intoxicating effect, just being closer made her hands clammy and her blood race. She tried to keep her composure, but Michael scared the shit out of her. She wasn't sure if he'd embrace her presence or strike her down where she stood. She clasped Luke's hand, taking strength from him.

Michael studied Luke and then Mary. "I see what I've been told is true. Luke, you have feelings for her?"

Gabriel intervened. "Michael, they just met. A crush, maybe, but no, my son knows what is needed of him and knows not to get too close."

"Gabriel, let the boy answer. Luke?"

"I do."

"Good. Mary, do you feel the same?" Mary nodded in agreement and squeezed Luke's hand. "There is a prophecy that Lucifer is not aware of. I had hoped to use it to obtain his defeat. I think now we'll get the chance."

"What prophecy?" Luke straightened his back.

"The day shall come when light and dark become one.

Joining together and bringing with it, a new army. One that will serve all of mankind. This is why you are drawn to one another. Our Father wanted this union to defeat the son he once loved . . . the one who betrayed him. Luke and Mary are the dawn of a new union.

"Mary, it will be a struggle when you reach fulfillment to keep yourself on the path of the light. But I feel, as do most of the souls in Heaven, that you can overcome this legacy of darkness. You have a great power inside you, learn as much as you can during the training sessions over the next few days and listen to your heart. Both you and Luke will need each other. Rely on each other's strengths to overcome the weaknesses. You will be successful. After all, look at who your mother is. How could you not succeed?"

"My mother?"

Michael turned to Gabriel. "This child doesn't know?"

Gabriel shook his head. "I just found out last night that Araqiel kept it from her. He told her she had died in childbirth. I felt it better to break the truth to her when we could sit down and explain everything. That is, until you let it out just now, Michael," Gabriel said reproachfully.

Michael turned to her. "Mary, let us finish here and then I'll sit and explain this to you."

She nodded, but inside her stomach was writhing. She was going to find out about her mother, all the things her father would never tell her. She would finally get answers. Trying to focus on Michael, she quieted her mind and concentrated.

"My friends, the time is upon us. We will all be called to play our part in stopping horrors that could bring the destruction of man. Our allies have found out that Astaroth will be here soon." Michael looked around the room. "I can see the fear and doubt in your expressions. Maybe a bit of training should begin now with insight into who you will be facing.

"Lucifer's legions have punched a hole in Hell and are being aided by misguided humans who believe that the devil will reward them. These fools make our job harder. We will teach you to recognize his disciples. They could be anyone you know. Each carries a distinguishing mark they receive after pledging themselves to the Dark Prince. It is the mark of the beast—a small tattoo of a serpent encasing the hand of God.

Luke spoke up. "Is the tat on the same place for everyone?"

"No. And it isn't recognizable as anything other than a tattoo to the untrained eye, but to you it is certain death. If you encounter one of his disciples, you must not hesitate to strike them down.

"Our brother Uriel will arrive today. He is the archangel of light and fire and possesses an uncanny talent for problem-solving, we will need his strategic skills. While we are waiting, Peter, Gabriel, and a few other senior angels, will begin your combat training. You will soon learn to fly.

"Tomorrow night we will complete the first step of fulfillment by gracing all of you with your wings. This is a gift that usually does not come until your eighteenth birthday, but it's become a necessity.

"Mary, the issue of your wings is in debate. Some among us remain wary about granting you this power, and until they can agree, you will need to wait.

Mary released a heavy sigh and looked to Gabriel, who smiled reassuringly. She wanted so much to do the right thing and abiding by what the angels said seemed to be a good start, so she nodded in response.

"Thomas and Vincent, your jobs will be to scout around town for new faces."

The two elder angels had been a couple for many years and the community often looked to Vincent for his wisdom.

Michael continued. "Abaddon and Abezethibou have likely brought their own minions with them. I would like to identify as many as we can before tomorrow evening. Do not approach them, no doubt the demons have informed them we know they're here. Let them relax a little, we'll strike when the time is right.

"Cassie, you'll teach Becca. Test her gift and see if she can home in on our enemies." Cassie nodded.

"That about does it. You all know what you have to do. I know it's late and you must be tired but there's little time for rest as long as the Dark Prince is a threat. Let's get started." Michael clapped his hands. "Mary, will you come sit with me? You can start your training after we talk."

The busy floral pattern on the couch screamed out to Mary. Like an overgrown garden waiting for a weary traveler to lose their way, it reached for her. She hesitated; her body frozen to the sculptured carpet beneath her feet.

"I promise, I won't bite." Michael waved for her to sit down.

Luke turned to leave but Michael stopped him. "You should hear this, too."

He sat down beside Mary, and she eased back, dropping her shoulders. Strength in numbers felt better than facing this alone.

"Mary, do you know anything at all about your mother?" Michael began.

"Only what my father told me. She died when I was born and that I'm half demon like him."

"Well, that's partly true. You are half demon, but your powers are greater than those of a once fallen angel."

"I'm confused. If my dad was an angel, then why am I a demon and not half angel?"

"When your father was banished to Hell, it was his wish to consume the darkness. It changed him, and he welcomed it. He asked Lucifer to accept him as a demon, leaving any morsel of his former self behind. When he met your mother, he had already been granted his wish.

"Remember, Araqiel is an archdemon, you possess enormous powers, most of which you haven't begun to tap into yet. Part of that power comes from your mother as well. What your father told you is a lie."

Mary pulled away from Luke and scooted to the end of the cushion laying her crossed arms on top of her knees.

"Your mother didn't die. She is alive. Your father took you from her. She was betrayed by her closest friend and together, Araqiel and the woman brought you into hiding. Araqiel wanted you for an offering to Lucifer. When you reach fulfillment, he intends to present you to him. Your mother is Lilith, the first woman of Eden."

Mary pressed her palms to the sides of her head—brain shivers. The pressure building up like steam in a tea kettle, the vibrations left her ears deaf to everything else. *Lilith*, how was that even possible? She remembered picking up a book from the library once. Filled with stories about religious myths. Everything she had read about Lilith was folklore, not real. And if she was real, she wasn't good. The stories depicted her as self-serving and tyrannical.

"Mary. Did you hear me?"

"Yes. Lilith."

"No. I said she's been looking for you for a very long time."

"But she's not good, she's a horrible person. How could she give me all this power and the side of me that is with the light? It doesn't make any sense."

"Fabrication and gibberish. Those are all things created by the archdemons to suppress the truth. Yes, Lilith did leave Eden, but God forgave her. She redeemed herself a very long time ago. She has been fighting on the side of the light for many millenniums.

"In the beginning, Lilith fell in love with the archangel Samael. They were very happy together for centuries, until the day she met Araqiel. He became obsessed with her, and when she wouldn't return his love, he tricked Samael and had him sent to Hell. Lilith lay with him only after he agreed to free

Samael. After she became pregnant with you, she went into hiding."

Mary couldn't help herself; the questions were burning inside her. "But how did I wind up with my dad?"

"Araqiel found her just days after you were born and kidnapped you. She has been heartbroken, searching for you ever since. Araqiel hid you in the cloak of darkness for most of your seventeen years. He's used his human followers and a barrage of lowly demons to keep you just out of her reach. He has also had demons searching for Lilith with orders to kill her. If she finds you, it'll disrupt his plans to present you to Lucifer. Samael was sent back to Heaven for his safety, where he's been preparing for Lucifer's attempt to rise up."

Mary asked accusingly, "He just abandoned her? How could he do that?"

Michael gently took her hand. "He wanted to come back for her, but we are soldiers in an army, and he was under orders. Lilith understood. Your mother is strong. She knows you will be called on to assist in Lucifer's war against humanity. For her to come to you would have put you both in grave danger. When the moment is right, she will find you. It is just a matter of time."

Mary wanted a few minutes alone. She needed to take all this in. In one night, she went from being a seventeen-year-old girl with powers she didn't understand, to a defender of Heaven, with a fallen angel turned demon for a father and Lilith for a mother. She massaged her temples. The skull cracking thump in her head incited crashing waves of nausea in her gut.

Michael rose and said, "I'll give you a few minutes to yourself."

She mustered a smile while swallowing back the acid in her throat.

"I need to get out of here, I feel like the walls are closing in," she whispered in Luke's ear.

Outside, the morning sun had risen, laying warmth to the

foliage waiting to drink up the light. The training had begun, and the back and side yard resembled the playground at the park, but instead of soccer or baseball, the teens were engaged in hand-to-hand combat, and defensive actions. Mary navigated to a settee in the far corner of the property with Luke sticking close by.

She sat down and took in the menagerie of adults and teens, all too busy concentrating to realize they had a spectator. Luke plopped down beside her.

"I want to hate him so much right now. What he did to my mother and me, lying all these years. You don't know how many times I wished for a mom. And now I have one—somewhere."

"I know."

Mary glanced up. The vagrant grey and white clouds sauntered in from the east painting the sky. She shivered.

Luke saw this and briskly rubbed her hands with his. "Any warmer?"

"Uh huh." She peered up into his eyes. She could melt into them, just stay together in silence, and let the world go on with whatever it needed to do.

A firm squeeze on her forearm yanked her back to reality. It was Jason.

"Hey, you two, we don't have time for this. They want you practicing with the rest of us. When the sun sets, Uriel will be here, and they'll start the beginning of the fulfillment. We get our wings soon. Crap, sorry Mary." Jason sighed.

"It's cool. I'm just happy they're trusting me enough to let me stay. I could never do the things my father is capable of, or at least I'd like to think I'm not."

"You're not," Luke said confidently.

Mary smiled, the corners of her mouth slightly rising. He had so much faith in her. *Please don't let me betray him,* she heard the words ring in her head.

The bearable temperature of a sleepy morning sun allowed

for the practice of physical maneuvers but when the heat intensity grew in the afternoon, the training switched to perception alteration and mind control. One of the older teens was able to focus on a large donut shaped float, gliding it back and forth across the pool.

Luke was especially good at syncing his mind and body to perform as one. His fluid movement that made him the star quarterback spilled over to angel training.

A glimmer of visions filled Becca's mind like a chaos of photographs thrown on the floor. A few gave her the full pictures but some just bits and pieces. Sometimes it would help if she could concentrate on something as simple as a white sheet pinned to a clothesline, flowing in a soft breeze. As the sheet flew up, sinister faces would appear, stealing her breath.

They were all learning so much in a short time.

After several hours of continuous training, Michael called for a break. The kids needed to eat something and prepare for the next phase—flight.

Gabriel set paper plates and plastic utensils on the tables in the backyard and Cassie made sandwiches and salad for everyone. As an archangel, Michael did not require food to sustain his life, but he sat and broke bread with everyone. A custom the earth-bound angels had adapted to.

Halfway through the meal, Uriel arrived.

"It's about time, I was beginning to think our great strategist couldn't find his way to my house." Gabriel squeezed Uriel's shoulder.

"As usual brother, you're a bounty full of laughs." Uriel smirked.

Michael cleared his throat, and the room grew silent. "Brethren, I'd like to introduce you to Uriel."

"Hello. I wish we had more time but we don't, so let's begin." Uriel's tone was assertive.

"I know Michael had mentioned followers of the Dark

Prince. Don't be fooled by their human appearance. They are every bit as diabolical as their demon counterparts. They will stop at nothing to please Lucifer. We will be sending out search teams of humans who are loyal to our army. Their sole task is to seek out and destroy this threat."

Luke interjected, "But they're human. Can we persuade . . .

"No. They made a choice to serve evil and we are at war."

Luke squared his shoulders and glanced at his dad. Gabriel tilted his head.

Uriel continued but Luke turned away. This angel wasn't at all like his dad or Michael. His tone chilled the room, and Luke didn't like it. His thoughts were interrupted when a brush along his hand caused him to jump. Mary's breath grazed his ear. "Look up."

The three archangels had been too absorbed in their plans to notice the change in the sky from benign to ominous, but she did. Past a large bottlebrush tree in the yard, in the distance, steel grey clouds rolled quickly toward them. They were moving ferociously, eating up every shade of blue like a wild animal dining on its prey. The shadows rolled in faster and faster without the aid of the slightest hint of wind.

"Dad. Dad!" Luke yelled.

"Son, we're busy here. I'll be there in a few minutes."

"No, look." He pointed toward the clouds that had now grown black. Thunder rumbled, and a blazing axe of lightning chopped the sky. Michael jumped to his feet with Uriel and Gabriel following.

"He's coming." Michael cried out. "Everyone get ready. There's no time."

"Who?" asked Luke. "Who is coming?"

"Astaroth."

Scrambling to their feet, they quickly abandoned their food for battle. Uriel lined up those who would be receiving wings and Gabriel armed adults with weapons. Michael stood ready.

The ground shook ferociously, followed by a gut-wrenching boom. The new soldiers of Heaven struggled to remain standing while the angels and archangels opened their wings and took flight.

The clouds parted as if they were torn apart by a mighty hand. Barreling down from the horizon they came—ten, twenty, thirty or more demons, each more horrifying than the next. Luke's mouth dropped open, and his eyes widened, their misshapen bodies and distorted faces stopped his heart. A cold shiver shimmied up his spine, he knew he should move but he couldn't. The nefarious creatures from hell were as assorted as any group of humans, but these weren't humans. Protruding eyes, slits for eyes, or no eyes, flaps of flesh for ears, or horns where ears should be, muscles wrapped around charred bits, hooves for feet, legs of enormous width, their bodies resembling more of pieces and parts randomly constructed, and each one wearing a face of pure demented evil.

Three colossal beings were in the center. Their charred flesh taut over their bulging arms and legs. Their mouths were void of lips, only large holes with exposed gums and long pointed teeth. Their blood orange eyes glowed with the intensity of the summer sun on the barren desert, and a single horn protruded from each bald forehead. The larger of the three abominations took point, with a ring of fire circling his chest. They tightly surrounded Araqiel.

Mary's father struck Sebastian Ryan, one of Gabriel's oldest friends, with a sword. The angel plummeted to the brown patch of desert below and lay motionless in the center of the yard.

The largest guardian from Hell appeared to be the leader. Mary guessed him to be Astaroth. Michael weaved rapidly through the league of demons, knocking them back with ease. He maneuvered himself above the center demon. Two more swooped in, joining forces with their monstrous brother.

Michael battled Abezethibou, the archdemon from the park,

while Uriel focused on Abaddon. The others stayed on the ground, fighting the low-flying agents of hell. Luke grabbed Mary by the arm and ran to his mother. Cassie used her body to shield Becca, pushing her further back away from the turmoil.

"Stay here with my mom. He's after you," he told Mary.

"I'm just as strong as you. Stronger," she protested. "I can help."

"I know, you can probably kick my ass, but if this all hinges on you in the end, we need to keep you safe now."

But it was too late. Astaroth spotted her and began his descent. Luke eyed Michael as he abandoned his fight with Abezethibou and followed close behind him.

Gabriel pleaded to the heavens, "I beseech to you my brothers, bestow on them their first gift." Luke winced when a raucous boom drilled into his ears. The clouds exploded revealing the majestic ball of fire and light.

Luke cleaved his chest, his heart dry of blood, he began to shake. A brilliant hue of gold emanated from within, illuminating every inch of his body as it began to rise from the ground. He looked up at his friends, smears of butterscotch glittered across the atmosphere. He shouted out to Jason as their bodies flopped backward like the rag doll Becca carried with her as a toddler. Floating closer to the heavens, their will was no longer their own.

Legions of low-level demons soared toward their intended prey, but they were left dazed when their efforts were thwarted by an unseen shield protecting the teens from harm.

A sphere of lightning descended from the clouds, settling down among the boys and Karen. Tentacles of electricity extended from the center and encircled each teen. Luke tried to call out to his dad, but the cry stuck in the back of his throat. A ripple of fear stroked his spine as he instinctively put his hands out in a defensive manor. The current twined its way around his hands and then creeped along his arms. His body tensed, a raging heat taking his flesh prisoner as it mapped its way down his torso and legs. Finding his voice, Luke roared a welter of cries before convulsing and then resting calmly in the clouds.

Fluttering his eyelids, he slowly peeled them back. Raising his head, he scanned the clouds for his friends. Huge cream-colored wings with flecks of tan and gold sprouted from their backs, with each downward stroke, the feathery protrusions slightly twisted, keeping them in flight. He scanned the azure canvas for the ball of light, but it was gone, leaving behind an almost feral sense of confidence. Taught muscles strapped along his newly sculptured physique, pulsated with strength.

He hovered for a moment, trying to get used to the motion of the flapping wings. But practice would have to wait, he gritted his teeth and hoped instinct would lead the way.

Michael had fought Abezethibou and ripped his left wing off, leaving him fallen and unconscious. But Astaroth had descended. He had Mary, Cassie, and Becca cornered.

Luke, Michael, and Gabriel flew toward him, surrounding him as the others continued fighting demons both in the sky and on the ground. Carnage and destruction lay below his feet. Demons swooped with precision, wielding daggers, swords, and taking aim with fiery bows and arrows. Some of the new angels had been injured. Uriel summoned Rita Peterson, who healed them as fast as she could. Still, they were doing well for their first battle. They were strong and smart and some of their opponents had started to fly away.

"Give up, Astaroth. You are surrounded and we will never let you have Mary," commanded Michael.

"You fools. The Dark Prince is coming, and he will get what he wants. You are just delaying that which is inevitable. Why not save yourselves? If you give her to me, your death will be quick and painless."

Michael laughed. "You are as stupid as you are ugly. I will cut your heart out and hand it to Lucifer personally. It is you who had better be on his way."

Astaroth looked around at his scattered demons and the motionless Abezethibou. Abaddon was still fighting, but Uriel quickly winning. Astaroth knew he could defeat Gabriel and Luke, but Michael was to be feared.

"I will be coming for you Mary, and the next time, Michael will not be there to stop me. Beware, Michael. Your time is coming." Astaroth ascended into the sky, followed by Abaddon, and their brothers of hell.

Uriel and Gabriel dismembered Abezethibou and flew away to bury his pieces in various parts of the world. One less demon, especially an archdemon, meant one less worry.

After Rita had healed the injured, Michael called a private council with the senior angels. Then they summoned everyone to gather in the living room. Michael gazed around the room before delivering their latest strategy.

"We know Lucifer's disciples will be relentless in their pursuit for Araqiel's daughter and we have an idea we want to discuss with you Mary."

She took a step forward, separating herself from Luke and giving Michael her full attention.

"I think the best way to keep you safe is for you to go into hiding."

Mary inhaled and held the breath for a few seconds before releasing the heavy burden inside of her. "I don't want to leave but if I really am the key to us winning this, then I get it."

"No." Luke intervened. "We can keep her safer here."

"We don't know that. In fact after today, I'd say keeping me here puts everyone else in more danger." Mary stood firm.

"I understand your hesitation Luke, and when Becca's sight reaches its potential, I believe we'll get answers we need to fight this war but until then it's our best plan to keep Mary safe." Michael turned his gaze to Mary and nodded.

"When do I go?"

"Almost immediately." The raspy voice, carried from the front door, was alluring.

The entire room hushed, and Mary stood completely still, unable to move. Inside the frame of the front door stood the most beautiful woman she had ever seen. Her ebony eyes framed with wavy brown hair cascading down to her hips, complimented a strong posture, and confident stance.

"My daughter." The sound of her voice melted like butter off the lips.

Mary felt the room go dark. Luke caught her as she fell. They brought her to the couch, where she opened her eyes and turned to the stranger.

"It's okay, don't be afraid," Lilith said. "You must have questions. But for now, we must go."

"Now?" Mary's eyes widened.

Luke grabbed Mary. "You can't take her away."

"I'll be okay." Mary whispered.

"This is stupid AF. I'm going with her."

Lilith looked up at Cassie, who bit her lip, but nodded in agreement.

Gabriel went to his son and embraced him.

Michael reached out and placed his hands on Luke's shoulder.

"All right, boy, go with Mary. Give each other strength, you're going to need it. Lilith will hide you, but the demons will be hunting you. When we know their plan, we will rise and fight. There is no time for long goodbyes. Go."

"I'm scared of me," Mary whispered to Luke. "What if nothing can be done? What if I turn no matter what? All of this would be for nothing. You should stay here."

"We do this together. I'm not worried. I know who you are." He pushed a strand of hair from her face.

As Mary let the events from the past two days wash over her,

her limbs grew cold with dread. Then she tilted her head and met his eyes. She almost believed what he said was true.

Luke went to his mom. Hugging her as her tears rained onto his shoulder, he whispered his good-byes. Becca struggled to hide her emotions. Her eyes betrayed her. He clasped her hand and gently rubbed the back of it with his thumb before letting go. Standing with Mary at the front door, he took one last long look at the family he was leaving behind. The acids in his pit reminded him of how much love he'd taken for granted in his short seventeen years.

Jason approached and embraced him. "Don't worry, bro," he said. "We'll win. They won't know what hit them. You and Mary stay safe."

The couple walked outside, where a large black SUV with dark tinted windows waited. Lilith sat in the front seat with the driver, who never moved his gaze from the road ahead. Luke and Mary quietly climbed into the back seat. As the car pulled away from the curb, he looked back wondering if he'd ever see home again.

FOUR

Luke gazed up toward the ceiling of the warehouse. Skyscraper sized open windows lined the south wall. He scanned his surroundings for a way up. If he could reach them, he could crawl out. Hopefully, Mary and Lilith were safe somewhere outside, waiting for him.

They had gotten separated when Astaroth surprised them at the motel. Lilith had set an impenetrable cloak over their room, but somehow, he still found them. They barely got out unscathed. Well, somewhat unscathed. Luke's side was still burning from the sharp claws of Astaroth's fingers.

He lay still while the water trickled down the side of his face, landing on the collar of his shirt. He clenched his jaw, sealing his lips to reassure silence, but it sounded like thunder every time a drop hit the soft cotton. It was silly to think he could be betrayed by a droplet of his own sweat. His heart thrashed against his rib cage—he needed to slow it down. The demon's hearing was astute; it would give away his location as easily as if he stood and shouted his position. He closed his eyes and concentrated on Mary. Her beautiful face: his mind locked on the image and his body relaxed at the thought of the girl he loved.

His heart slowed. *Thud, thud.* A long, quiet breath. He had been practicing, and now it was time to put it to work. *Tap, tap, tap.* The rapid beating calmed to nearly a whisper, *tap—tap—tap—silence.* He had done it. He had slowed his heartbeat to the point that it was barely audible even to the trained ear. His heart wouldn't betray him. It was one of the new talents he had learned since discovering his true self and leaving his family months ago.

"Come out, boy. It is no use hiding. You are trapped and we both know you haven't the power to defeat us. I will make a bargain with you. Surrender, and I promise, when I kill your family, it will be quick."

His left wing was still healing from his last encounter with the agents from Hell, so flying was not an option. *Think Luke, there has to be a way.* He pressed his back further into the boxes stacked on the steel shelving behind him. Astaroth was searching aisle by aisle. But where was Abaddon? Those two always traveled together, and Luke hadn't seen or heard him since he ran into the warehouse. As the boxes pushed back, his eyes widened. If he could steady himself by standing on the lower box, he might be able to push the boxes back on the shelf above so he could gain footing and climb up. If he made it outside, there'd be a significant drop to the ground, but he was willing to risk it. He stepped up and grabbed the edge of the metal structure with one hand while pushing on the boxes up above. They were heavy, but strength was one of the bonuses of being an archangel. As he inched the box back, it created enough room for him to pull up and stand. Laying his arm on the bottom of the shelf, he hoisted himself up. He was in position just as Astaroth rounded the corner. Inching between the two boxes, the warm, metallic liquid painted his lips. Unlocking the steel grip of his jaw, he swiped his mouth with the back of his sleeve.

Side stepping across the metal, he winced as he slid deeper between the towering shields.

"I told you, boy, do not make this difficult. It will be far less painful for you and your family. We will find all of you and we will win this time." Astaroth groaned. "The longer this takes, the more enjoyment I will get as I pull your wings apart one golden feather at a time."

Luke clenched his fists as his blood boiled, running rapid to fill the chambers of his life force with a venomous surge. He needed to stop. This is exactly what Astaroth wanted him to do. Placing his hand on his chest, his words didn't betray him ... *Ramona Lane.*

"Have you ever seen an angel who has been de-winged? Probably not, you're too young in your experiences. It is not a pretty sight. So sad and pitiful. No reason to live, actually. That is why I make sure to kill each and every one of them after ripping out their pride. I'm really rendering them a service. You see, I am not without mercy."

Astaroth came further down the aisle, stopping no more than a foot away from Luke. Tightening his stomach muscles, he fought to contain the volcanic eruption in his belly. He couldn't slow his heart for much longer. Eventually, the lack of oxygen to his brain would cause him to black out. The pressure had already begun rushing to his temples as he pressed his head further into the stiff surface for balance. A chill stroked his spine when a second set of footsteps stomped toward him. Abaddon came barreling down the aisle, echoing his arrival.

"Come with me brother, there's another way." Abaddon commanded.

"The boy is in here somewhere and he is injured."

Luke gingerly leaned to his left, a sliver of the two demons visible through a sideway glance. Abaddon turned and whispered into Astaroth's ear. He nodded and followed.

Luke's chest heaved with each contemplation of breath,

bringing his heart back to full pumping capacity. He swung his legs over the side and jumped down. Lucky for him, he would get to exit through the door. Cautiously, he crept toward freedom. But what was so important that it took Astaroth away from his prey? *Oh, no . . . Mary.*

Luke punched the steel door, knocking it off the hinges onto the ground. He scanned the parking area for any sign of the two agents of Hell—nothing. He wanted to call out to Mary, but knew it wasn't the wisest choice. If they did have her, they'd be prepared for him. If they didn't and she answered him, then he would hand her location right over to them.

Ambling to the edge of the building, he prudently stretched his head around the corner. No one.

Wait. Behind a large grey sedan, he thought he saw something move. He stayed behind the wall, cloaking his location. Squinting his eyes, he knew it could be a trap but . . . red Chuck Taylor sneakers—*Mary.* If he went to her, he would risk exposure with nothing to shield him from the demons' view. He decided it was the only way to get to his love. Without another thought, he rushed to her. The fear coursing through his veins was matched only by the wind rushing by him as he moved with the speed of an archangel. In seconds, he was by her side. Mary's eyes filled with tears as she realized who it was, and they collapsed on the ground in a tight embrace. Lilith was in the car pumping the gas as she turned the key in the ignition. "Holy crap, thank heavens you're okay," she called out.

Luke nodded. "It's good to see you, too."

Lilith slammed the driver's door and the couple quickly jumped in the back seat. They'd lost their driver to Astaroth's rage about a month ago. The poor man had been crushed like a leaf under the sole of a leather boot.

"I think I almost got this." Finally, the engine turned over and Lilith slammed on the gas.

"Where to now?"

"We're going to meet up with—" The car skidded out of control, jostling the three of them forward. Luke peered out the back window and saw the two demons, Astaroth and Abaddon, flying above them a few yards away. He shouted to everyone to hold on, as he watched a fireball of lightning release from Astaroth's palms. Lilith had a tight grip on the steering wheel as she tried to steady the car. The vehicle swerved back and forth across the highway, narrowly missing the side-rail. Mary unbuckled her seat belt and swiveled completely around, facing the rear of the machine.

"Mary! Buckle yourself. Another jolt like that and you'll fly right out of the windshield." Luke reached over to grab the seat belt, but Mary pushed his hand away. She twisted her head around; her eyes were like two black pools—just like the first night they met. Her grey skin and puffed cheeks contorted the beauty she had been only seconds ago. It didn't resemble the girl he loved at all. With a wave of her hand, Luke was pinned back to the seat. The more he wiggled to get free, the tighter the grip became.

"Mary. Stop. Let me go."

She paid no attention to his plea. Instead, she glared directly at the two demons. An explosion of darkness stole Luke's breath, as the rear glass shattered sending a trail of shards behind them.

It was in the late evening and thankfully, there were no other cars in sight. Lilith managed to gain enough control to pull over to the side of the road and watch as Astaroth and Abaddon were rocketed straight up into the sky, propelled about a hundred yards back and slammed into the side of a large, free-standing billboard. Quickly, Lilith threw the car into gear and bolted back onto the road. She reached up and adjusted the mirror to get a look at the two demons. They were motionless on the asphalt.

"That's not going to stop them, but it did buy us some time. Thanks, Mary." Lilith reached for the knob on the dash and turned the radio on. Luke's body relaxed and the constraints of the seatbelt loosened. By now, Mary had re-buckled herself and leaned her head on the window, gazing out. Luke inched his hand towards hers and clasped it. She turned her head further toward the window.

"Mary, look at me."

She kept herself turned away.

"Please, look at me. I want to see your eyes."

Cautiously she allowed her eyes to meet his. Luke smiled. They were once again a warm brown. All of the pain and anger was gone from her face. She was Mary again.

"You're back."

She let go of his hand and tilted her head away from him.

"Yeah, for now, but I need to get a handle on this."

Lilith interjected. "You will. The place we're going to, they're going to be able to teach you how to manage your transformation. If you can manipulate and own it, you'll have a better chance of helping us and yourself. Both of you are in the procurement phase of your fulfillment."

"Procurement? What does that mean, Mom?" Mary startled herself. That was the first time she had called Lilith Mom since they met.

Lilith could see the uneasiness in her daughter's eyes as she viewed her in the mirror. Even she was stunned by Mary's reference. Hoping to hear the words one day but knowing it would take time, she didn't press it. "Procurement is when you'll develop new skills—gifts. Your angel strength is one of them. Mary for you it's your demon half. But other abilities, both physical and mental, will come. Once your procurement is complete, you'll have achieved fulfillment."

"Mental? What's that mean?" Luke raised a brow.

"Many things, it just depends on which ones are chosen for you."

"Telekinesis? Could I move things with my mind?"

Lilith grinned. "If the celestials bestow that on you, then yes."

"Cool. I want that one."

Luke shifted in his seat. His back felt stiff, but it wasn't from the long car ride. He'd injured his wings fighting one of hell's demons and it hadn't fully healed yet.

"I gotta tell you, six months ago the concept of wings were beyond my wildest thinking. But now, once you get them, it's a bitch when you can't use them."

Lilith frowned. "Yep. I wouldn't personally know it, but I've heard your dad grumble a few times back in the day. He was grounded once for about a month. His injury was deep after an especially brutal battle with one of Lucifer's disciples, but yours isn't that bad. You should be healed in a few days."

"I hope so. I feel powerless without them. I couldn't get to you back at the warehouse. I barely got myself out of there. My strength is really growing, but they can still throw me around like a football."

"A football, huh? You sure are your father's son." Lilith peered through the rear-view mirror to the back seat.

Luke leaned his head against the glass, the scenery whizzing by made him a little dizzy. He realized it'd been a while since they ate.

"Can we stop for a bite? I'm not feeling so hot."

"I'll pull into the next gas station. You can grab some snacks. I want to stay on the road. It won't be long before those two demon asses wake up, and I want us to be a good distance away."

Luke reached out and placed his hand on Mary's knee squeezing it slightly. He smiled. She inched closer and put her hand on top of his.

He was happy they were together, but he really missed his family. He wondered what they were having for dinner and then chuckled to himself. How weird that something so simple can seem so important now.

"Hey, you doing okay?" Mary asked.

"Yeah, why?"

"You got a faraway look."

"Nah, just thinking about home."

Mary sighed. "Yeah, demon dad has a way of creeping into my thoughts too. I mean, it wasn't all bad with him. I guess I have a love/hate relationship." She punched his arm.

"Hey, what was that for?"

"I don't know, just because." She grinned.

Luke rolled his eyes. He knew she was trying to lighten his mood, distract him from thoughts of his family with humor. It kind of worked—for a minute.

Luke reached out and tapped the back of Lilith's seat. "I'm gonna call my parents when we stop. I want to see how everyone's doing and if Becca's headaches eased up."

Lilith peered through the rearview mirror and nodded.

None of them had a cell phone. When they wanted to communicate with their allies in Boulder City, they bought a disposable phone and discarded it as soon as the call was done. Luke thought this was a bit extreme. How would they trace a throw away phone? But he heeded his dad and Lilith and kept with the plan.

By the time they pulled over, Luke was in dire need of a bathroom. He leaped out of the back seat and asked Mary to meet him inside. Lilith pulled the red covered nozzle from the pump and slid it into the car. She handed Mary her green lizard-print wallet, some of the stitching was frayed and the edges of two pennies threatened to squeeze their way out if given the right opportunity. "Grab me a bag of chips and a Pepsi," Lilith ordered over her shoulder, turning her attention back to the numbers spinning behind the dusty plastic face of the gas pump.

Mary looked back over her shoulder. "Will do." She grinned to herself, her mom was literally the first woman ever and she wanted a Pepsi. How normal. But she's not. She's thousands of years old. "My mom, first woman and junk food junkie," Mary whispered

Luke splashed cold water on his face before grabbing a paper towel to dry off. His ears perked up; he could hear Mary as if she were standing right beside him. He laughed; Lilith did enjoy her Pepsi. Hmm, angel hearing was kind of cool.

He joined Mary in front of the candy bars. She had a real sweet tooth, something Luke thought was cute. She could sniff out chocolate from a mile away. He grabbed a few bags of cookies and chips and stood next to her.

"Can't decide?"

"Nope. They're all good."

"Then get all of them." Luke leaned into her.

"No. I can't, that would be ridiculous."

"I don't know, the way Lilith talks, we'll be driving for a while. You might need all of them. We don't know when we're gonna stop again."

Mary laughed heartily. He loved her laugh; it had been a long time since he'd heard it. Quickly, he started grabbing every candy bar off the shelf. She tried to stop him, but he managed to fend her off and race to the counter. He threw them down, the clerk's eyes widened at the bounty of sugar. Luke stretched his neck to the right, scanning the display of disposable phones, he snatched one and threw it on the counter with the pile of sweets.

Luke smiled at the clerk. The corner of the man's lip twitched in an almost smile before he turned his attention back to the job at hand.

Mary grabbed a six pack of Pepsi and water and met him at the register.

"You two must be really hungry."

They just grinned and paid in cash, leaving without any further conversation. No need to engage with this stranger. It was safer for him that way. Lilith was waiting in the car, as they jumped in and threw the snacks on the seat between them.

"Uh, if you two are ready to go, could I please have my soda and chips? I'm hungry, too, you know."

"Oh, sorry." Luke handed them over and then opened the phone packaging. After activating it, he dialed his house. His mom answered.

"Luke, is that you?" She sounded concerned.

"Yeah?"

"Are you all right? It's been weeks since we heard from you. We were beginning to get worried. Your dad's been in contact with Michael. He's waiting for you. Have you reached him yet?"

"We're on our way now. Sorry you were worried. We had a few run-ins, but we're doing great. My hearing is getting really strong, and Mary's powers are growing too. How's Becca? Did the headaches stop?"

"For the most part. She still gets one from time to time. But the stronger she gets, the weaker they become. It won't be long before her body adjusts, and she won't have to deal with them anymore."

"Oh, great. Is everyone else okay? Is Dad around?" Luke really needed to hear his dad's voice.

"Yes, they're fine. They're all training very hard. You should see Jason. He's a real warrior. I'm sorry, your dad isn't here. He's gone with Peter to meet with a scout about a new demon that was spotted in town. And you? Procurement? I know it's a lot."

"It's good. Lilith explained it all to us. I really wish they'd give Mary her wings, though. It would make things easier for us."

"Michael and Ariel are working on it. From what I understand, they've almost got everyone in agreement."

"Listen, Mom, I don't know when I'm gonna be able to call again. Tell Dad and Becca I love them and remind Jason of the promise he made me. Okay?"

"What promise?"

"He said he'd take care of things until we return." Luke felt an emptiness in his chest. He wanted to go home and be with his family and friends. It would be so much better if they could face this together.

"Don't worry, he is. I don't think you'll recognize him when you get back. Please stay safe and keep in touch when you can." Cassie's voice cracked and Luke tried to reassure her.

"I will. Don't *you* worry, Mom. Lilith's amazing, and we're getting stronger every day. We'll be home soon." Luke hung up the phone. He had said what his mom needed to hear. But he had no idea when they would be home or if they would ever make it there again. The demons were relentless, and even though Mary was growing equally as capable, she wasn't really in control. Luke flipped the switch to lower the window and threw the phone onto the passing highway—his connection to home broken. A heavy weight sat on his chest, and he swallowed hard. Darkness was creeping up behind them and he wasn't so sure they could outrun it this time. He laid his head on the window and closed his eyes, a temporary reprieve from the reality of impending death.

Mary admired her mom's reflection in the rear-view mirror. It felt strange earlier when she blurted out the word *mom*, but it was also comforting. She had never thought there would be a day she would get to say that word to anyone. After all, her father told her that her mother had died. What reasons did she have not to believe him? All these years, she'd had no clue her mother was alive and who she really was. Time wasted, but no more.

The sun rose above the horizon spraying amber rays through the window and nestling along Lilith's long brown tresses. Glittering in the sunlight, they graced her shoulders like silk. Mary was in awe of her mother's beauty. She wanted to spend hours just sitting somewhere and having normal mother/daughter conversation. She yearned to do all those things she had seen other girls do with their moms. But she was different and so was her mom. A fear rose from her belly, waking up the acids in her pit. What if she did lose control one day? What if . . . *no*, it's not gonna happen because she won't let it. She's the driver of her own destiny and some evil AF reject from Heaven isn't gonna change that. Maybe one day, they could find their own normal. For now, she was just happy to have her mom. Even though life had changed dramatically in a short time, knowing her mother made it all worth it. Lilith lifted the hair off the back of her neck, twisting it with one hand and exposing her long neck to the breeze coming through the window. Mary noticed a partial tattoo peeking out from the back of her hairline. She wasn't able to make out what the design was, and it didn't feel like the time to ask. Maybe she just didn't want to know, because from her perspective, the tip of art showing reminded her of a snake. Mary wriggled; her spine held prisoner from a cold chill. No, she was helping them to safety, to Michael. Mary pulled her dark thoughts back into the light.

Hours passed and she was growing uncomfortable and cramped in the back seat. Luke had been quiet for a while and the silence was beginning to agitate her. It gave her mind too much time to wander and that wasn't good when the only thing she could think about was Araqiel and how he'd deceived her for so long. Grabbing her legs, she began massaging them and then kicked off her shoes and stretched her feet. Then, she rotated her neck and leaned forward, letting her head and arms drop down. When she rose up, she saw Lilith watching her in the mirror.

"You okay?"

Mary loved the tone of her mother's voice. It was a soft hoarseness that captivated the ear.

"Yeah, just feeling a bit cramped. Do you think we can stop and walk around a bit?"

"I'll get off at the next exit. We can take a bathroom break and you can stretch your legs."

"Oh, great. Thank you." Mary smiled back at her. She still

felt awkward when addressing her. Her inner voice wanted to shout, I love you, thank you for rescuing me, but the outside— what she let Lilith see—was a totally different persona. As she sat back in her seat, she yearned for the day this would be behind them. At the same time, however, she doubted that day would ever come.

The exit sign read, Huntington Beach. They were in southern California. She rolled the window down and took in the aroma of saltwater and humidity. It brought her back to her childhood. Some of her fondest memories with her dad were at the beach. The Atlantic Ocean had a greener, sometimes grey cast to it. This ocean was bluer.

Lilith pulled into a Chevron station and decided to fill the half empty tank while Mary stretched her legs. Luke heard the commotion and woke up.

He peeked out from the back seat, Mary was doing the best yoga impression she could, given the fact she was standing beside the car somewhere between home and their destination.

"Hey, you feel like a walk?"

"Heck yeah, my legs are all achy."

They hurried across the wide highway to the waiting briny blue. Barely audible over the passing cars, Lilith called out, "Be careful!"

Golden rays cut across the azure blue sky, warming Mary's arms, and relaxing the ache from hours spent cramped in the back seat. Gulls screeched overhead, swooping toward the water, dancing to the song of the waves breaking on shore. Luke and Mary ambled along, drawn to the symphony unfolding in front of them.

Their feet pressed deep into the moist sand, as the ocean waves climbed and fell, showering them in a cool mist. The icy foam swarmed over the tops of their feet as it retreated to rejoin the deep. Mary jumped back and Luke laughed.

He bowed and curled his arm up into the air then extended

his hand. She took it and twirled, the landscape racing by her side. For a moment they were two goofy teens again.

In the distance she heard her name. She didn't want to hear it. She didn't want to know who it was. She just wanted this moment.

"Mary! Luke! Get back now." They broke free of each other and turned to see Lilith flailing her arms furiously. She was pointing toward the sky. The couple turned around to see a mass of black and red in the distance coming straight toward them. Luke grabbed Mary's hand and yanked as they barreled toward the car. Mary kept looking back as they raced across the street. She squinted, and then stopped. No, it couldn't be. Not him.

"Mary, get in." Luke pushed her in.

"It's my dad." Mary didn't budge.

"What the fuck?" Luke followed her gaze, the outline becoming clearer as it neared. The broad shoulders, wavy dark hair, black jacket with red t-shirt, everything the servant of Lucifer had on at their last encounter when he loosened his grip on Luke and let him plummet to the earth. A mix of anger and fear stole his breath for a split second. It was Araqiel. Forcing the air into his lungs, Luke pushed Mary into the car and Lilith took off with the speed of an Indy 500 driver.

"I know a safe place." Lilith gripped the wheel.

She made a quick right turn into the nearby hills. Luke grabbed onto the door handle to keep from jostling any more than he had to. He turned to check on Mary, her gaze concentrated on the rear window and preoccupied with the threat growing closer by the minute. So much, she'd forgotten to buckle her seatbelt.

"Mary . . . seatbelt."

"Huh? Oh." She buckled up.

Taking a sharp right around the oncoming bend, they traveled deeper into the hills and the comfort of an actual neighborhood. Maybe it was a false feeling of security, but it eased the tension in Luke's grip on the door handle.

There were large custom homes on both sides of the road. Some were tucked behind thick foliage and if not for the roof tops, you wouldn't know they were there.

"I have a close friend here. He can shield us."

She continued to maneuver the car through winding roads until they came to a long, secluded driveway that sloped down into a covered parking area shrouded in the midst of tall pine trees. She got out and pulled a key from her purse. She walked over to a little box mounted on one of the posts. Putting the key in, she lifted the top open and revealed a button. Lilith pressed the button and the car—along with the three of them—jolted then descended.

Lilith turned to the backseat. "It'll feel close, but don't worry. We have plenty of room. It won't be long."

"Get a load of this," Luke whispered to Mary.

Large white stones with black symbols adorning each rock reminded Luke of the Hebrew alphabet. He'd seen it during religion class in grade school, when a visiting priest recalled his time in Jerusalem.

The slow movement of the car-evator, a name Mary coined in her head, made it easy to soak in the beauty. She hesitantly reached her arm out the window. Letting her fingertips kiss the stone, the cool dryness felt tantalizing, a contrast to the stuffiness of the car. Part of her thought she should be weary, after all, the space left barely enough room for the car to fit. One tremor and they could easily shift into the rock and then fall to injury, or worse—death. She had no idea how far they were traveling underground. But none of that bothered her, and she couldn't figure out why.

"Does this feel strange to you?" She glanced at the walls.

He reached for the stones. "No. Oddly, it feels . . . like home."

"Yeah. Like home."

The platform gently came to a halt, and they found themselves in a large underground garage filled with antique cars and motorcycles. LED lighting flooded over the shine of the waxed steel, gleaming brightly throughout the structure. Luke squinted. Mary got out and walked over to her mother who was standing in front of a '32 Ford Victoria—black like all of Ford's original cars.

"It's beautiful. Where are we?" Mary inquired.

"A very dear friend. He should be down here in a moment." Lilith caressed her daughter's hair and delighted in how much she resembled her and not her father.

Mary switched her attention to Luke, he eagerly moved through the aisles separating the cars. His eyes grew wider with each new model he investigated. She grinned; it was cute how excited he was. A sudden thud from behind the wall directly in front of her and Lilith pulled her gaze away. A hidden door opened and out stepped a muscular guy who appeared to be about forty. Dressed in faded jeans, flip flops, and a crisp, white T-shirt, his dark locks were pulled back in a low ponytail, cascading halfway down his back. He walked straight up to Lilith and gave her a tight embrace and a kiss on the cheek. Lilith returned the embrace and the kiss.

"Mary, Luke, this is Samael, my . . . beloved."

"Wait, what? Samael? Lilith . . . Mom." She cleared her throat. The M word escaping her lips for a second time. "I thought he was sent back to heaven?"

"He was sent here to help us a few years ago. He's been hiding me from Araqiel." Lilith turned to Samael. "He found us, love. I think I lost him on the way here, but I need you to cloak us."

"No worries, my sweet. He will never find you here." Lilith laid her body into Samael's chest, and he kissed the top of her head.

Mary hated to ruin the moment, but the question slipped past her lips. "Samael, how come you didn't come to Boulder City with Michael? I mean, if Lilith was going there and you were helping her, shouldn't you have been on the trip with us? We could've used the brawn."

"Hey, what am I the dope sidekick?" Luke screeched.

Mary rolled her eyes.

Lilith pulled away from him and faced her daughter, hands on hips, she glared. But Mary ignored her. It was a simple question, and she was tired of everyone's deflection of their situation. If she was the key then she needed, no deserved, answers to the burning questions she's been piling up ever since she found out who she really was.

"And while I'm thinking about it, how come you have so many cars? I mean, you fly, right?"

Samael glanced sideways to Lilith. "Yes, she is definitely your child. As tenacious as the day is long. Mary, I didn't come with Lilith to get you because I was ordered by Michael to stay here. One thing you should know, Michael is our general. We abide by his word. As for the answer to the second question—I really like fast cars."

Mary couldn't help but laugh. She tried really hard to tighten her lips and push it back out of existence. But the idea of an archangel racing around Los Angeles in a Lamborghini amused her.

"Please, join me upstairs. I'm sure you're all hungry, I'll start dinner while you wash up. You can put your things in the guest rooms and then relax." Samael waved them on toward the staircase.

"Thanks dude," said Luke. "I'm starving for real food. Lilith has a thing for gas stations and chips."

"I was trying to save us from a horrible death. Excuse me if fine dining wasn't on my list of important things to do."

"Point taken."

Samael interjected, "I guess you guys are pretty worn out and a home cooked meal would do you all some good."

"Yeah, a good home cooked meal would hit the spot."

"Who said anything about good?" Samael raised a brow.

Luke rolled his eyes and Samael laughed. "Don't worry kid, I'm pretty decent in the kitchen.

FIVE

Luke rubbed the sleep from his eyes. Hues of gold pierced the double pane glass reflecting a small ballet of light on the stainless-steel top of a nearby desk. He liked this bedroom. The qualities of an urban loft in the middle of the southern California hills, it was the coolest blend of city and country. Samael had given Mary a room down the hall. Understandable, but not what Luke would have chosen. He threw off the top sheet and shuffled over to the window. The painted cement felt slick on the heels of his feet. He had gotten used to wearing his boots all the time. This was the first time in months he'd actually slept without them.

He grabbed his pants that were draped over a corner chair. The warmth of the room felt good. Safe. Cracking the door, he peeked down the long hallway to see if Mary's door was open. It was. Sauntering to her room, he felt the light following him from the skylights along the length of the hall. He must have been too wiped-out last night to notice them. It reminded him of being under the spotlight for the one and only school play he performed in. He only had two lines but he messed them up every time. It was the beginning and ending of his stage career. He chuckled to himself.

Mary was making her bed, her back turned when Luke rapped on the door interrupting her solace. She swirled around to face him.

"Oh. You startled me."

"I'm sorry. I missed you. I wish they had let us stay together last night."

Mary's cheeks flushed. It always threw her a little off balance when he said things like that. Part of her wanted to melt into his arms and share every part of herself with him, but the other half still had trouble believing. Her dad wasn't a warm man. In fact, she never really remembered getting any compliments growing up. Luke was open with his feelings. She loved it, but that didn't make it any less embarrassing for her. She usually handled it by using a very strategic move—she ignored him.

"We'd better get downstairs. I bet Lilith is probably up by now and I'm starving." She put some socks on and grabbed a lightweight cotton shirt out of her bag to layer over her camisole.

"Uh, yeah, okay. I'm hungry, too."

Mary relaxed. He let it go. Another thing she adored about him. No pressure.

Following the salty aroma permeating through the house, the teens wandered into the living room which connected to the kitchen by a spacious bar and stools. Samael stood at the stove scrambling eggs while Lilith sat on a bar stool at the counter looking at her laptop. A plate of warm bacon beside Lilith begged to be eaten, so Luke snatched a piece and took a bite. Turning, he was immediately drawn to the cornflower blue sky that stretched across the large picture window on the back wall of the living room. He took a step forward but retreated immediately. Last thing they needed was for demon dad to spot him in the window.

Samael noticed Luke's anxiety. "What's up kid? You don't like the view?"

"It's not that. What if Araqiel sees me?"

"That won't happen. The entire hillside is protected from demonic forces. They can see the hill, but not the houses. To them it's just Southern California rolling greenery."

"How?"

"A cloaking spell from an old friend, Mary LaBoccetta."

"Will she be helping us?"

"No. She lives back east, and she's got her hands full with another kind of evil right now."

"Shit. Monsters are like everywhere."

"What, you thought Boulder City, Nevada, had exclusive rights to the underworld?"

"Well, no, but . . . never mind."

Mary plopped down on a bar stool next to her mother and leaned in to see what was on the screen. A map of the California coastline.

"Are we leaving today?" Mary shifted the plate of bacon.

"No. Samael spoke to Michael this morning. He is waiting for us at the secure location. We'll wait a few days and then leave. It'll give you two time to train with Samael and enjoy the anonymity the hills have to offer before we put the bullseye on our backs again."

"Lilith." Luke had sat down next to Mary. "I don't mean to play devil's advocate—no pun intended, but damn, how are we gonna get there unnoticed? Nothing seems to have worked so far. Those demon ogres always manage to catch up with us somehow."

"I realize you're frustrated," Samael chimed in. "We're all waiting for the go ahead from Michael. As soon as we know, you will . . . .promise."

"I spoke to my mom earlier, before we got here."

"How is she? I haven't seen her in such a long time." Samael smiled at the mention of her name. "We used to be quite the force. Your dad, mom, Lilith and I. Indestructible at one time. We'll get it back, though. We have an army growing once again and Lucifer will be defeated for good this time."

"I don't know, dude. That sounds good, but from what I've seen so far, they're not goin' down easy." Luke grabbed a plate, scooped a spoonful of eggs onto it, and sprinkled them with cheese. "These things are non-stop. They don't care how many of them die. They just keep coming at us over and over again."

"They bleed; therefore, they die. We will win."

"I hope you're right, because the alternative is something I never wanna see."

Luke wasn't paying attention when he reached for another slice of bacon, he bumped Mary's hand when she grabbed for the same piece. His eyes darted from the last well-done strip of goodness to Mary who was biting the corner of her lip. Lingering for a moment, his hand softly brushed hers and then retracted.

"Go ahead, you take it." He released his hold.

"You sure?"

"Yup."

"Thanks." Mary blinked.

Luke took his plate and stepped out onto the balcony off the living room. He needed to feel a connection to nature. He missed the open space of Boulder City. Leaving his family was rough, but the thought of Lucifer winning made that pale in comparison. Hell would exist on Earth. There would be no more civilization—not a recognizable one anyway. Lucifer would torture and enslave anyone left alive. Anyone who was gifted with death would suffer a brutal one. Any surviving angels would be made to pay for helping the humans—including Luke. It was hard to think of himself as anything other than human—but he wasn't anymore. His fate—and that of his family—would be terrifying if they lost.

His chest rose with a deep breath, inhaling the scents that gave him hope.

The rest of the morning and early afternoon they spent relaxing. Lilith would've preferred training, but Samael convinced her a movie binge never hurt anyone.

It was three-thirty when Samael left for the store to get supplies. Lilith was still busy mapping out a plan for travel. She wanted them ready for anything. Tracing the route between Samael's house and Michael's location, she studied the terrain. Which roads were less traveled and the best place to hide while moving toward their destination. She created three separate routes she considered the least exposed and also the most direct.

Pinpointing motels and other lodgings along the way, she created a list with addresses and saved it on her phone. Finally, she narrowed the field of stores where they could purchase supplies. They weren't about to walk into a Walmart and be overly exposed. Small, independent gas stations and convenience stores would be the logical choice.

Although Lilith made it clear that neither Mary nor Luke could leave the hills, they weren't confined to the house. Mary sat on the couch with her legs propped up on an ottoman flipping through channels. Boredom seemed to fuel her every movement.

Although Luke thought bored was a hell of a lot better than dead, he recognized they'd both had enough of the four walls and HBO. Getting out of the house would be good for them.

"You want to go out for a walk? I need to get out of here for a while." Luke grabbed a bottle of water out of the fridge.

"Sounds good. It's a little too quiet right now." Mary grabbed her MP3 and slid it into her back pocket.

Lilith looked up from her laptop. "Stay close. And don't venture out beyond the hills." Her eyebrows were knitted together and her mouth pursed. She disapproved of them leaving the house but wouldn't fess up to it. Luke didn't care, he needed to do something that didn't involve being boxed in.

"Don't worry. I'll take care of Mary."

"Yeah? And who's gonna take care of you?"

Luke wanted to argue but nodded instead. He needed to pick his battles with Lilith. She was strong, clever, and the driving force that kept them alive, but he felt she had no clue of what he was really capable of. He had changed over the last several months. Being hunted by a relentless group of archdemons will do that to someone. But she was Mary's mother and about an eternity old, so silent agreement was his best response for the moment.

The front door was stubborn, a side effect of the humid California weather—a direct contrast to the desert summers he grew up with, Luke gave the door a firm jerk and it opened. He inhaled the sweet scent of Primrose, filling his nostrils with delight. Emerald, green needles clung to the branches of the majestic pine trees towering over the magnanimous forestry. It was definitely different from the grey-green landscapes back home. An orchestra of birds concealed amidst the dense trees lulled mother nature with their cheery tune, and calling the young couple further into the menagerie of topiary delight.

"It's so beautiful here," Mary said softly.

"Why are you whispering?

"I feel like if I said it too loud, it'll all go away."

A large root from a Blackwood Oak lay in the path carved out by the wilderness. Luke took a wide step and unfolded his hand out to Mary, she raised a brow but took it.

"Feeling gallant?"

"I thought it might earn me some points. Did it work?"

"I'll let you know."

Mary noticed a large Praying Mantis boldly standing its ground a few feet away. A small beetle made the bad decision to cross its path and the carnivore struck before the poor scamper knew what happened.

"Hey, wanna practice a few moves?" she asked Luke.

"Where'd that come from?"

"Not wanting to be food for a demon."

"Sure, okay."

The teens took a fighting stance, Mary was the first to strike. With stealthy deception she reached for Luke with her left hand but swept her foot up and into the back of his knees. He fell on his ass but quickly hopped up, ready to resume battle. This time he engaged his divine power and leaped about ten feet in the air, coming down behind her. He got his right arm around her neck and pulled her to the ground. They both rolled, landing at the base of a tall pine.

"Now what?" he asked.

Mary turned her head to face him, a clearing in the forest a short distance away caught her eye.

"Now we explore over there."

Luke followed her gaze. Once again, he unfolded his hand to offer aide, but this time she jumped to her feet and grinned.

Stepping between a family of oak and dagwood, the bowing trees welcomed their guests. Glitters of orange and yellow peeked through the shade of their branches, illuminating a patch of deep, lush, St. Augustine. The teens folded down into the sweet smelling, bed of greenery. Mary slipped off her Chuck Taylors and squished the blades with her toes.

"It's damp, do you wanna get up?" Luke asked, hoping she'd say no.

"It feels good."

Mary lay back and nestled her head into the long, feathery blades. The clear blue sky weaved through the bough of the trees, painting strokes of blue between the vivid green.

Luke smiled to himself; she was peaceful—an emotion that

had been rare on their journey. He lay down beside her, moving his arm awkwardly to his hip.

She turned her head. "What are you thinking?"

"About home, this . . . all of it."

"Yeah, it's been a ride. And it's not over."

Luke pretended to take a picture with his fingers.

Mary giggled. "What are you doing?"

"Making a memory."

Lilith looked up from the latest route she had mapped out for their trip. Glancing over at the clock on the stove, she murmured to herself about the whereabouts of Luke and Mary. Wandering over to the panoramic window in the living room, she scanned the surrounding grounds for the two teens. Although she knew they were well hidden from Araqiel and his demon dogs, Astaroth and Abaddon, anxiety showered over her. She was writing a note when Samael came pushing through the kitchen door, arms filled with groceries.

"What are you doing, my lovely?" Samael dropped the bags on the counter and reached out for Lilith.

"I'm glad you're back. Did you see the kids outside when you pulled up?" She nervously pushed away and proceeded toward the door.

"No. Why?"

"They went for a walk, but they've been gone for a while. I want to make sure everything's okay."

"I'm sure they're fine. The demons can't get them here. They need time together. Don't you remember how we used to be when we were young?" He reached for her again, but Lilith pulled back.

"I do, but I need your help right now, not a walk down memory lane."

"Okay, babe. I see you're worried. Let's go."

Lilith ambled to the edge of the property and looked down the winding asphalt road. Nothing.

Samael waved her over. "Maybe they're down by the creek." Lilith grabbed his hand and they wandered through some heavy brush, pushing it back to make a path.

"This is really tucked away. How much further?"

"Only a short distance more. It's a remote clearing I sometimes go to, to gather thoughts. I'm not sure if they found it, but I think it's worth checking." He softly smiled.

"All I want is for my daughter to be safe, and Luke strung up by his heels for keeping her away from the house for this long. I didn't get her back after all these years, just to lose her because of some hormonal teenager."

"Hey, hold up. First of all, Luke isn't just a teen. He's the son of a very powerful archangel and happens to be one himself. He's not irresponsible. I think you've seen that proven several times over the last few months, or at least that's what you've told me. They're just on a walk and enjoying some shred of normalcy. For however short the time will be."

"I know. Everything you said was right. It's just, Samael —*she's my daughter*. I've waited so long to be with her. It's making me a little crazy."

"Nope. You were already crazy." Samael grabbed her and planted a kiss on her lips. "Do you remember that time we had to lose the entire Roman army because they thought you were trying to kill Marcus Aurelius?"

"I was. Philosopher, my ass! He tried to have his way even though he knew I was in love with you. He was a scoundrel. Historians can play him off any way they want, but I know the truth." Lilith stood straight back, shoulders square like she was ready to engage the enemy.

"Ah, there's the delicate little flower I love," Samael said sheepishly.

Lilith grinned. "I love you, Samael."

"I love you, too. My little warrior."

The ground beneath them succumbed to the warmth of the mid-day heat drinking up the moisture and, with it, their relief from the rising humidity. Luke didn't mind, he'd withstand any inferno just be close to Mary.

The teens shared earbuds and listened to some songs from Imagine Dragons. He turned his head from Mary to gaze up. He had never felt the kind of connection he did with her.

His eyes traveled back to the curves of her lean body. She was unaware of the beauty that she possessed. Living with the type of father Araqiel was, Luke was in awe of her ability to see things with such clarity. The angels gave her an impossible scenario and she accepted it. She had doubt, but also courage. Her eyes were closed, and he could faintly hear the words of the song she muttered under her breath. He grinned.

Abruptly, Mary shot up and the moment was broken. With one finger to her lips, she motioned for him to keep quiet. He tilted his head to focus his hearing on the vast forest, crunch . . . crunch, someone was approaching. He scrambled to his feet. The intensity of the unknown faded away when Lilith's call for Mary sliced through the air like a sword aimed at Luke's neck. She was close and the fear returned as quickly as it had left moments ago.

Luke's heart pounded, it felt like it would rip open his chest at any moment. He glanced at Mary; she bit her lip. Lilith came through the clearing and judging by the narrowed eyes and flared nostrils, she was pissed. Samael was a few feet behind her, keeping his distance from his volcanic girlfriend. He gave a silent shrug to Luke, both men knew it was better not to poke the lion. Or in this case, the protective mamma lion, and the cub she was recently reunited with after seventeen years of searching.

Lilith didn't say a word and just pointed toward the house.

Mary started to go but stopped. The one day they had a few hours alone together and Lilith was ruining it.

"I don't get you. You say we're protected here, and we were just listening to music and talking. Why do you always have to be so much?"

"Excuse me?" Lilith crossed her arms. "I'm too much? I'm responsible for keeping the both of you safe."

"In case you haven't noticed, Lilith, we both have way more powers and pretty much can get things done on our own. Have you forgotten I'm a demon?"

"Half-demon, daughter. But that's not the issue. The trouble is, if you think you're indestructible, you're gonna get yourself killed. And yes, you're cloaked here on the mountain but what if Araqiel sent a human?"

Mary blinked. The thought never occurred to her.

"Loyal disciples to Lucifer are everywhere."

Luke rubbed his brow. He decided to keep the peace.

"Sorry," he mumbled.

Mary let her gaze travel from her mother to Luke; she didn't apologize. Instead, she turned around and headed back toward the house, leaving an uncomfortable silence between them.

The home that welcomed them now felt more like a prison —with throw pillows. Mary longed for her old bedroom in Boulder City, even if it meant living with a demon dad.

Lilith cooked supper while Samael decided to grab a shower. The sticky humidity was not his favorite climate. Luke sunk into the couch and watched the ending of Die Hard, while Mary stewed from across the room on an oversized chair dressed in taupe microfiber and matching ottoman. The longer she remained silent the greater the pressure to blow. She was pissed off at her mother's lack of faith in her abilities. Yes, a normal average human being chased by evil beings, taking a stroll out in the woods for a few hours, could be daunting. But she was anything but average, and it was about time her absentee mom let it go.

She scooted out of the chair and walked into the kitchen.

"Lilith, I need to talk to you."

Lilith set the large spoon she was using to stir dinner on a small plate on the counter.

Mary interpreted her calm movements as a calculated play and geared up for battle. "Are we gonna talk or argue?"

"That depends on you."

Mary squared her shoulders and crossed her arms. "When are you gonna realize I'm not just some kid? I've proven I can take care of myself. I'm not saying I don't need help, but I've done seventeen years without you."

Lilith held her breath, the last remark cut to her soul.

"You need to ease up, you're suffocating me." Mary glared.

Lilith rubbed her forehead. Clenching her fists, she turned her back to her daughter to take a moment to choose her words.

"You're right. You did have many years without a mother, and I'm sorry. And you are not without your talents. But you are also my child and new to this world of demons and ogres. I will protect you whether or not you want me to."

Lilith stood firm. "We good?"

Mary's arms fell to her side, and she nodded. Hearing Lilith say she's her child melted most of the anger. It wasn't like she didn't already know this, but she now had the relationship she'd dreamt about all her life and maybe it was time to try and be a daughter.

Dinner was relatively uneventful. Samael put music on. His favorite Pandora playlist. It was nothing that Luke or Mary particularly liked, but it was his house.

Lilith, a vegetarian, cooked potato and carrot stew with kale and barley. Luke, a diehard meat eater, was surprised to find he actually enjoyed it. Something that pleased Lilith, based on the giant smirk on her face as he scraped his bowl clean.

"Not bad for a dish that doesn't contain one morsel of a slaughtered animal. Wouldn't you say, Luke?" She was giving him a hard time and Luke suspected it was because of what happened in the woods.

"Actually, I'm really surprised. It was one of the best dishes I've ever had. Maybe you'll make a vegetarian out of me yet." He flashed his teeth in a wide grin and then grabbed his plate to place it in the dishwasher. Lilith started to come back at him, but Samael intervened with a yank on her arm and pulled her into the living room to dance to an upbeat song that had come on.

Toward the end of the song, Lilith broke free and waved her hand for Samael to follow. Luke and Mary were just finishing the dishes.

"The two of you come join us at the table, we have a few things to discuss. We're going to be leaving soon, and you need to know this." Luke's set his elbows on the table and leaned in. "We've mentioned the people who will help us get to Michael, they're job will be to protect us."

"Who are these people?" Mary's voice was tense.

"The Order of the Guardians of the Gate. They're a secret society who have sworn their loyalty to God and to the protection of mankind. They're over two thousand years old, dating back to the days when Jesus walked the earth."

"How do you know they were here when Jesus was?" Luke asked.

"I was there."

"Oh, right."

"Watching, waiting, and moving about unnoticed. The coming days of war were foretold long ago, they chose their side and remained loyal throughout time. Now the moment has come for them to emerge from the veil of shadows. They will be helping us along the way. I'm not going to lie. This will be the most difficult part of our journey. Lucifer has sent a new legion of archdemons more powerful than we've encountered in the past. Many of our human allies in the east have already been slain. You'll both experience your procurement, the period when you acquire your abilities. As you take on each new power, you will have to learn how to harness it and use it against those who want to harm you. Normally, you would be guided through this process under the watchful eyes of the archangels. They're responsible for assuring you properly reach the end of Fulfillment and become the best possible warriors. But we don't have the time or the resources to do that now."

"What gate are these guys guarding?" Mary was tapping her fingers nervously on the table.

"The gate represents every passage between Hell and Earth. There are thousands of Guardians throughout the world. They watch for signs that the enemy has pierced a hole into this realm, then act quickly to close it. They are the first line of defense in this war. If they can't manage on their own, they call Michael."

Mary crossed her arms on the table and laid her head down.

Luke was still focused on what Lilith said about their training.

"You act like we haven't been training. We've been busting our asses for months and I think we've done pretty good so far." Luke got up from the table and leaned against the bar, crossing his arms. "When can we expect our powers to come? It's been months since I got my wings, and I can do a parlor trick here and there, but nothing like what you're talking about. I don't think slowing my heart is going to be pivotal in winning this war.

"And what about Mary? When does she get her wings? How much longer until she's proven her loyalty?"

"I know you're both anxious. Your gifts haven't been fully explained and you didn't have the time necessary to ease into them. Usually, your wings are the last power bestowed. These abilities are different for everyone but that's not to say some of you won't share the same powers. Luke, you've learned to slow your heart rate to the point of near death, and your hearing is better than any animal, which you share as well, Mary. She will get her wings when the council decides she should. You will get your remaining powers when your body is ready to receive them. Now can I finish?"

Mary and Luke shook their heads in agreement. "Samael, will you go get the weapon from the vault?"

"Sure thing." Samael walked over to a solid wall in the living room. From his pocket he withdrew a gold coin. Pressing the coin on the wall, he slid it up and down while chanting. "Mee-DEH-leht, le-DEH-leht." Then he stepped back, revealing the doorway, and disappeared.

"What was that?" Luke rushed over to the gaping threshold and started to go inside.

"No!" Lilith jumped up from the table. "Don't go in there."

"Why? And what was Samael saying to make it open?"

"It was Hebrew. The translation is 'door to door'. You can't follow him because it's a dimension that only selected angels can go to. A safe haven for items they don't want in the wrong hands. It's protected by enchantment. If you follow him, you'll be slain."

Luke backed away with a swift step and sat down on the couch. Wide eyed, Mary studied the opening from a confident distance. Her eyes darted from the outer threshold to the black space waiting for its next traveler. Taking a step, she bumped into the edge of the coffee table. She gripped the pillowy arm of the sofa to regain her balance. Steadying herself, she folded down to the couch and scooted next to Luke. "Angel land," she blurted out.

Samael emerged into the living room and as quickly as it had divulged itself, the doorway disappeared. In Samael's grip was a large, bladed dagger and scabbard. Luke stood as Samael placed the weapon in his hands. Feeling the weight of the handle and carefully running his fingers over the top of the blade, he admired its powerful beauty. The steel blade shined an impressive eight inches in length and two and a half inches in width. That alone was impressive, but it was the grip that caught Luke's eye. Crafted in gold, a small globe split in two equal halves by a precise black line capped the end of the unusual piece. Intricate leafy carvings mapped their way along the sphere adjacent to a four-inch shaft with three rings carved into the top, middle and bottom of the precious metal.

"Can I see the scabbard?" Luke carefully placed the dagger on a side table, then took the cover into his hands. Intricate embossed brass plates and rings adorned the front and sides. He ran his fingers along the inside of the sheath, the leather rubbed against his skin like sandpaper.

Scattered streaks of rich brown suggested someone recently tried to oil and preserve the ancient hide.

Standing, Mary reached for the scabbard. "It's beautiful."

"Yeah, it is." He placed it in her hands, his touch lingering.

"Okay, you two, let's focus." Samael hunkered down on the couch next to Lilith, who had just taken a seat. "Babe, why don't you explain exactly what the Guardians intend to do and what the dagger is for?"

Lilith ran her hands through her long dark hair and peered up, resting against the back of the couch. She took several deep breaths as she bounced her right leg causing a vibration in the floor. She obviously dreaded telling them and that made Luke nervous.

If he'd learned one thing about Lilith this whole time, it was that she didn't scare easily. Countless demons, archdemons, and Lucifer were trying to punch through from his conflagration of an existence, and she remained unfazed. But *this* was bothering her.

"As I said, the Guardians will be taking us the rest of the way. We will be traveling in underground tunnels known only to them, and primarily by foot."

"To where?" Luke didn't like the sound of this plan.

Lilith's gazed traveled toward the ceiling. "Near Portland."

"Oregon! What the hell? Are you crazy? Do you know how long it'll take us to get there by foot?"

Samael chimed in. "Approximately thirty-six- and three-quarter days. We'll rest for eight hours and move for sixteen."

"We'll be underground for over a month?" Luke ran his fingers through his hair.

Lilith stiffened. "Look, I know it sounds incredibly long and believe me, if there were another way, I'd be the first one on that train. But Michael feels it's too dangerous to have both of you top-side. It was either this or separate the two of you."

Mary sat quietly through the whole conversation. Luke wondered why she didn't have anything to say about this bizarre plan. "What about you Mary, what do you think?"

"The truth is, I don't care. Not to sound mean, but if it gets us to Michael, I'm all in. I'm actually more curious about the dagger. There's something you're leaving out. You're obviously uncomfortable talking about this and it isn't because we're walking. What is it?" Mary grabbed Lilith's hand and gently squeezed it. "Why is the dagger so important that it had to be concealed?"

"Your mom is just trying to protect you . . ." Lilith held up her hand before Samael could finish his sentence.

"My beautiful daughter. So strong and bright, I've missed far too many years."

"Okay, now you're just scaring me." Mary got up and paced around the living room. "What is it?"

Luke chimed in. "Lilith this is bull, just spit it out."

Samael stood and towered over him. "Stop. Can't you see this isn't easy? Have you learned nothing? You keep telling us both how much of a man you are, and yet you still possess all the qualities of a boy."

"The dagger is the only weapon that can kill Lucifer." Lilith picked up the scabbard and gave it to Mary. "Take the four outer rings and give each one a turn. Now twist the brass plate, underneath you will find a hidden compartment."

Mary did as her mother instructed. Her stomach flipping with excitement, she could barely keep her hands from shaking. Luke leaned in; her eyes were electrifying. He could see the anxious wonder as they grew larger with each turn of a ring. Mary took a breath as she slid open the brass plate. Underneath was a tiny compartment and inside that, a wooden locket. Mary's head bobbed up and her line of site went straight to Lilith.

"Open it. But be very, very careful."

The lid was latched with a thin piece of leather over a tiny brass hook. Mary unraveled it. She took one more glance at Lilith and then lifted it up. She stood calmly for a moment, staring. Mary's body shielded the item from Luke's view, and he was exploding with curiosity.

"Mary—what is it?" His voice cracked.

Mary reached in and pulled out a curl of dark brown fuzz, wrapped tightly with another thin piece of leather. "It's . . . .hair."

Lilith delicately took the strands from Mary and placed them back in the locket. She then set the scabbard down and grasped the dagger from the table. Firmly grabbing the handle, she twisted it. It finally broke free, revealing a hollow cylinder in the center of the blade. Lilith placed the locket in the cylinder and twisted the hilt back onto the dagger, concealing its contents.

"This is the only means to kill Lucifer, because it is the only one that contains a piece of Jesus himself. This lock of hair has been protected for over two-thousand years. I cut it myself, the day of his death. He told me to keep it concealed, and to prepare for the imminent war that would be forged between heaven and hell. If Lucifer knew of its existence, it could change the tide of events. Right now, he's cocky . . . confident. He believes there is no way that he can be harmed. He's focused on Michael and the other archangels. But the truth is, it will be someone far less grand who seals his fate and sends him back to Hell. Once he is defeated with this dagger, he will be permanently imprisoned. No archdemon or creature will be able to free him again.

"You see, the armament is not in the dagger itself. Alone it's just a dagger. The actual weapon is the hair. Several centuries ago, the Guardians forged the dagger to encase and protect it. Before that time, Michael had kept the locket safe in . . . *Angel Land*." Lilith exchanged glances with Mary.

Luke took a minute to digest everything they had been told. He looked at Mary, who remained quiet, wondering if she shared his awe about what she'd held in her hands.

Mary walked over to the large window and stared out to the forestry surrounding the house. With her back to them, she finally spoke. "Who's the person? The one who sends Lucifer back to hell?"

"Mary, please come here and sit down beside me." Lilith slid into the couch and patted the cushion next to her.

"Who is it?"

Luke nervously cracked his knuckles, knowing what Lilith was about to say. Judging by Mary's stiff exterior, so did she.

"It's . . . you." Lilith's tears pooled up as she reached for Mary. They slowly trickled down her cheeks, and when Mary didn't budge, she buried her face in her hands.

"How long have you known? Is this the only reason you came back? I've been conscripted to wield the weapon. That's why you have been protecting me. And that's why Luke's parents didn't want us together. You all knew I was doomed."

"No. That's not true."

"How long?" Anger cut through the room on the sharp tone of Mary's voice.

"Since you were born."

"What the hell are you talking about? You've known all along?" Luke's anxiety quickly turned to anger. "How can you do this to your own daughter?"

Samael grabbed Luke's forearm. "Let's you and me take a walk. I think this is between Mary and Lilith."

Luke resisted and stood erect, chin to chin.

"Oh, you do not want to go there." Samael's threat was clear, he was taking him outside for a walk.

Luke reached out and took Mary's hand. She pulled her hand free and in a gentle voice, she said, "Go."

Luke nodded. He would go for her, no one else.

Samael waved for Luke to follow him to the back of the property. As they rounded the corner of the house, an orange and pink hue painted across the sky bidding its farewell to the day.

A high pitched *keeah* danced along the airwaves, drawing Luke's attention. He stood scanning the treetops for evidence of the ear-piercing sound, resting his eye on a mountainous pine. The slight movement separated bird from branches and Luke caught the blur of orange talons from a Red-Shouldered Hawk.

Samael walked to about the halfway point of the backyard and stopped.

"Run at me," he shouted to Luke.

"Huh?"

"I said run at me. I want to see how fast you can move. Don't stop until you knock me down."

Luke tightened his jaw. "I'm pretty strong."

"Then show me. Wait . . . one more thing." Samael puckered

his mouth and blew; a strong wind with the tempo of a small hurricane nearly knocked Luke off his feet. He squinted and instinctively threw his hands up to block the wall of air. Cocking his head, he fought the stinging salt of wayward tears. He pushed against the harsh wind and channeled all his strength to his legs. Cutting through the blast, it felt more like he was trying to walk through a river of wet cement.

Samael lifted a hand to the sky creating a loud crackle across the twilight canvas. A bolt of lightning nestled in his hand like a sword. With the twist of wrist, small jolts of electricity fired off like bullets. Luke raised up his left forearm to protect himself, each strike sizzling through his flesh.

"What the fuck is wrong with you?" Luke shouted.

Samael lowered his hand and rested it by his side. Closing his mouth, the wind immediately dissipated.

"You are going to war, and you need more training. While we are here, I intend to give it to you."

Luke filled his lungs with a deep breath and then vigorously released it. "Again."

***

"Tell me everything. And I mean *all* of it. I don't want any sugared down version or what you think I can handle. You owe this to me." Mary glared into Lilith's dark eyes. They weren't as piercing as they normally were. The whites had been painted with strings of red, drawing attention to the sheen on her cheeks.

"Please believe that I've wanted to tell you since we first met. Michael didn't think the time was right. You had just learned who you were, and the more vulnerable you were, the more defenseless."

"Ah, but I've never really been defenseless, have I, Mother? I mean, we all know what I'm capable of. Is that why I was chosen? Because I'm evil, just like my father . . . like Lucifer?"

"No. You were chosen for the completely opposite reason. It's your light. You are the only one who could get close enough to fool them because of the darkness you possess. But your light. . . you will lead us to victory."

"When you say, 'fool them', you really mean Lucifer, right?" Lilith turned away from her daughter.

"I'm not stupid. A dagger has to be used in close proximity. I'll need to be close to Lucifer to stick it in him." Mary wasn't backing off.

Lilith nodded her head in agreement. "When you were born, I was so happy. It didn't matter to me who your father was. I had this beautiful little girl, and you were half of me. I wanted to sweep you away and teach you everything. I never wanted you to grow up with him . . . have you so close to all that darkness. When he took you, I searched endlessly. I never stopped. The prophecy, as it was told to me is this . . . when the child of light and dark is born, she or he will have the power to right the wrong and imprison the Dark Prince for all eternity or . . ."

"Or what?"

"If she or he chooses the darkness, they can free the devil forever. However, I believe Araqiel knew about this prophecy long before I was pregnant with you. In fact, I think he specifically chose me. He knows my relationship with God was repaired centuries ago. He knows I walk the path of the true light and he knows the power I possess. He orchestrated the coming of this prophecy to earn the praises of Lucifer. What he doesn't know is the prophecy of you and Luke. In order for you to be successful and turn your face away from darkness, you had to find the one thing that would ignite your light. Give it the strength to suppress the dark side and use it to fulfill your destiny. Michael came to me right after you were born and told me of the prognostication and the role you would play. If I could have spared you this burden, taken it on myself, I would have."

Lilith collapsed into the plush cushions of the couch, letting them devour her.

Mary squirmed. The heat rising from her belly had to be pushed back. Electrical impulses coursed through her veins, and she clenched her fists to hold on and keep the demon at bay.

"Let's just get on with it." Mary's tone was once again sharp, her words slicing their way through Lilith's heart. That's what she intended anyway. Right now, in this moment, she could feel the darkness flowing through her and she needed it. It protected her from the emotions that could consume her, swallow her up and leave her to make mistakes. There could be no room for those if she would be dealing with the prince of darkness. She needed to be strong, clever, calculating and above all, removed. But it was still her mom, and in there lay the conundrum. Pushing out a long, slow breath, she relaxed her fists and let the anger go.

"Tell me what I have to do."

"Please, a minute."

Lilith got up and walked to the kitchen sink. She pulled her hair back, turned on the faucet, then cupped the water in her hands before leaning forward and rinsing her face. Patting it dry with the kitchen towel, she forced a half-smile.

"There will come a time that you will have to win their confidence. Convince them you've chosen the dark. I'm not sure exactly how or when this will happen. You will know when the time is right. You will go with them, live with them, and become one of Lucifer's loyal followers. Your father will be so overwhelmed to have you back—that his plan is working. He's always believed your dark half is stronger. It will work to your benefit. After Lucifer has risen and you are to secure your place by his side, that's when you will strike. Patience will be of great importance."

"What about the dagger? How will I hide it?" Mary chewed her lip.

"You won't. We can't risk them finding it. Samael will return it to hiding and when you feel the time is approaching, we'll work out a way for you to contact us. But Mary, Luke can't know about the plan. Samael will tell him that it will have to be you to pierce the dagger into Lucifer, but he will not tell him the details. His emotions are running high, and he could make a mistake. His impulse to protect you will most assuredly interfere with this plan going smoothly."

"Smoothly?" Mary made a fist and hit the side table with such force, it shattered. Splinters of wood showered to the floor. "Nothing about this shit is going to be smooth. As for Luke, you don't get to say what I can and cannot tell him. I'll decide." Mary turned toward the window again and caught a glance of her reflection. Her eyes were black as two sacred scarabs. Behind her she saw the round eyes and gaping mouth of her horrified mother. It was the first time she had witnessed her daughter's transformation. This was enough to pull Mary back to herself. Quickly pivoting, she faced Lilith. "It's still me. Don't be afraid."

"I'm not afraid. You're my baby. I could never fear you. It was disgust you saw in my face, not fear. Disgust for your father for giving this to you and keeping us apart."

"So, then, why all this running? If I am to be with them, why not let them catch me?"

"Because as evil as Lucifer is, he is even smarter. If this were too easy, he would know you were deceiving him. We have to make it look good. You will be taken by legions of Lucifer's army somewhere between here and Washington. That's the strategy and that's the part Samael won't tell Luke."

"I need time to think. I'm going to my room. Tell Luke I'll talk with him in the morning before the Guardians arrive." Mary ambled down the hall; all her energy drained by the reality of what was ahead. How was she going to hide this from Luke? These words played over and over in her head until she reached her room and collapsed on the bed. Hopefully, the morning would bring her answers.

———

Buttery rays sliced through the topiary of giants, glistening like fairies on the basil, green leaves. Lilith scouted the forest searching for the two men, she found them at the end of the property line, Samael sat on one of the two lawn chairs and Luke lie on his back in the grass with his bent arm shielding his eyes.

"Mary's gone to bed. She wanted me to tell you she'll talk to you in the morning."

"Is she okay?" Luke shifted to his feet.

"Yes. She's just very tired. It's been a hard day." Lilith sat down on Samael's lap. "It's getting dark, you should come in."

"No argument here. I'm beat." Luke wiped the back of his neck.

"I could use a few cookies. A man needs to stay strong." Samael flexed a muscle.

"Well, you're not human, you're an angel. And I doubt cookies are the food that's going to help. But okay. I'll see you back at the house."

Lilith made a left-handed remark about guys having bottomless pits as she walked away.

"Samael, how is this all gonna play out? I mean, if Mary's the one who has to kill Lucifer, how is she going to be able to get it done? He's never going to let her get that close to him. They know she's chosen the light. Araqiel would have told them."

"I can only tell you that if Lilith says there's a way, we need to follow her lead. You need to have faith and trust in her. She speaks directly for Michael, and he knows what he's doing." Samael stood up statuesque and proud.

"I wish I could be as certain as you." Luke slumped into his chair. "I don't want to lose Mary. Why can't I just do whatever it is? Why does it have to fall to her to send that bastard back to Hell?" Luke's eyes watered and he turned his head away from Samael. He didn't want him to see the extent of his fear.

"It just can't. Let's go and get some rest. You can talk to Mary in the morning. We have a long journey in front of us, and the Guardians will expect us to be ready."

"We? You're coming?" Luke felt a surge of confidence.

"Most assuredly. There's no way I'm sitting out on the chance to dance with the devil and see him fall flat on his face." Samael flashed a wide grin. "Come on, my stomach is growling for some double chocolate chips."

Luke peered back at the yard; Samael had leaned the two chairs against the side of the house—the way his dad used to nag him to do. He really missed his family.

The rest of the evening remained uneventful—even freakishly normal considering what they were preparing for. A handful of cookies, a few television shows—though Luke barely watched—and then bed.

As he lay in the dark room, he tried to envision a world where the prince of Hell had control. The room felt warm, but the thoughts that ran through his mind left him shivering.

Doubt can be a dangerous interference and that's what Luke had. Why did Mary have to be the one? How could she fulfill the prophecy and kill the devil? It didn't connect. He knew there had to be a missing a piece. He tried to focus on something pleasant, focusing on the memory of lying next to her in the woods, the air thick with the smell of pine and jasmine as the sun blanketed their bodies in warmth. He could almost feel her touch again as she reached for his hand and clasped it with hers. For a moment, life was perfect.

Six

Sweet Home Alabama, blasted from the alarm clock. More of Samael's music. Luke reached to shut it off, accidentally knocking it down between the side table and the bed. His hand scrambled along the floor like the tentacle of an octopus after spotting his morning meal. The sound carried down the hall to Mary's room and it was only a minute or two before she came barreling through the door. Luke was hanging over the bed.

"Really?" Mary folded her arms and took a stiff stance.

"What? I was trying to shut it off." Luke was balancing on one arm and looking up at her while still hanging off the bed.

"Don't you think it might be easier if you just got off the bed and picked it up?"

"What's the fun in that?" Luke was trying to get her to crack a smile, but it wasn't working. "Sorry I woke you up."

"You're impossible. I'm getting dressed."

Luke smirked, she was straining to keep a straight face, but her lips betrayed her as they curled ever so slightly at the corners. The moment was brief as a heartbeat, then she tacitly chuckled before leaving the room.

He grabbed his clothes and slipped into the bathroom to shower. The hot water rained over him. Cascading down his back, his shoulders relaxed. The calm before the storm, he thought.

Refreshed, he turned the water off and stepped onto the plush bath rug. Wrapping a towel around his waist, he stumbled, knuckling the brushed nickel towel bar his feet slid from underneath him and he careened down to the edge of the tub.

Luke startled as he looked up and saw two men standing in front of him. They were barely audible but clearly engaging in a conversation.

"Hey, who the hell are you? What are you doin' in here?"

They didn't acknowledge him.

"I said, what the fuck do you want? Where's Mary and Lilith?

Luke's pulse raced. He jumped up, the room grew darker, and his head spun violently. Dry heaving, he grabbed the shower door and glanced back at the strangers. That's when he noticed it, staring into the foggy mirror they had no reflection.

"JFC, what's going on?"

Inching forward, he cracked open the door. The flow of cool air ushered in, relieving some of the nausea. He looked back, trying to focus on their voices but they spoke in a tone less than a whisper. He thought he made out the name Michael or Mary, something with an M. Oh hell, it could have been McDonald's for all he knew. Then the interjection of a third voice, this one clearer and louder—Lilith.

"Hey, Lilith, what's up? Who are these guys? Are they the Guardians?"

She didn't answer.

He closed his eyes and focused on their words. Then slowly, he opened them. Falling back, he caught himself before he hit the ground. He was no longer in the bathroom, instead he was in Samael's living room.

"I think we're making progress." Lilith turned and locked eyes with Luke.

He looked over his shoulder, no one was there. Wait . . . could Lilith see him?

"I think it would be better if you were dressed. Don't you?"

"You can see me?"

"Yup. Every bit of you."

Luke sheepishly wrapped his towel tighter. "What's going on? How come only you can see me?"

Samael looked toward Luke, his eyes ricocheting around, but not focusing on him. His brows pinched as he looked back to Lilith. "Is it Luke or Mary?"

"Luke." Lilith grinned. "Go get dressed, and when you come down, I'll explain everything."

"Uh . . . how? I don't even know how I'm doing this." Luke's voice cracked. He was feeling unsteady with this new power.

"Well, how did you find your way down here?" Lilith asked.

Luke's mouth gaped open.

"So, I guess you have your answer."

Luke nodded halfheartedly and then he was gone.

He found his body sitting on the edge of the tub in a catatonic state, his ghostly projection hovered a few inches away. Luke reached out his hand slicing into the corporeal shell.

"Weird," he mumbled.

Inching closer, he closed his eyes and pushed his spirit past the flesh, rejoining body, and soul. Squirming as if to shake off the experience, he shot up and looked into the mirror. He wasn't sure what he was looking for or what he'd find, but it was just him. Huffing out a deep sigh, he quickly dressed and raced down the stairs.

This time he got a better look at the two strangers. The taller man's broad shoulders and brawny chest complimented his barely visible sculpted biceps. His square jaw and high cheek bones were clenched tightly like he needed a beer or maybe a date. Trim cut, dark brown hair matted to his head like a helmet. He eyed Luke with emotionless brown eyes. The smaller guy looked about as dangerous as a kitten . . . with bows . . . and a cuddly teddy. Short, round cheeks, and a tiny, pouty mouth. His black locks were disappearing, and the crown of his head could serve as a beacon on a cloudy day.

His mind spun with questions but before they could pass through his lips, Mary emerged from the patio door. She had been out on the deck and the sun had given her cheeks a red glow.

"Hey what's goin' on? What happened?" Mary's gaze traveled from Luke to Lilith and then the two strangers.

"What makes you think something happened?" Lilith took a sip of the diet coke she had in her hand.

"Well, for starters, you're all clustered together. And everyone's staring at Luke. What the hell?"

The shorter man cleared his throat and shook his head in disapproval.

"You mustn't make frivolous comments concerning hell, Miss."

"Okay, who's the doomsdayer?" Mary's words were sharp, but Luke had to laugh a little. The name fit the guy.

"This doomsdayer is Octavio. The other gentleman is Rufus. They are two of the best Guardians here on the west coast, and they will be by your side the entire journey."

"Are there more of you coming?" Luke asked.

Octavio raised a brow. "More of us? No."

"Well, that's soul sucking."

Octavio narrowed his eyes. "I do not understand what you mean."

Mary grinned. "He means wouldn't it be better to have more Guardians for protection?"

"The Guardians are all over the world. Just because it is only Rufus and I with you it does not mean they are not working with us. The order felt we would be sufficient to aid the plan."

Luke rolled his eyes. "Exactly what is the plan? Because this bits and pieces crap has to go."

The two men exchanged a glance and excused themselves before leaving the room.

"Hey, wait . . . what the . . .?" Luke called out.

A few moments later they emerged with a large leather satchel. Rufus set it down on the floor and opened it. He pulled out several maps and spread them out in front of Luke and Mary.

"These maps represent the routes we will be taking under the cities. I want both of you to look at them. Memorize each one with complete clarity."

Luke looked up at Rufus. "How? There's no way."

Rufus responded in a neutral tone, "One of the talents you both possess is photographic memory. Once your mind's eye sees something, you will never forget it."

"Uh, no." Luke shook his head.

"Well, that might be true." Mary slid over to the maps and began studying them. "I've always had a great memory. I never thought of it as anything special. Maybe you've just never realized it. Come here, just look at the maps."

Luke scooted next to Mary. He studied a portion of the map and then looked away. Mary quizzed him on it, and he nailed the whole route.

"You see, you got it." She grinned.

"How come I never knew this?" Luke looked up at Lilith.

"Probably because you weren't really paying attention. It wasn't important to you. But it's important now, and you know it."

Rufus interjected again. "Study them, know them inside and out. When you're done, we leave."

Rufus and Octavio sat at the table leafing through a local

newspaper while Lilith and Samael packed a backpack with supplies. A plethora of crackers, peanut butter, water, anything that didn't need cooking. Samael added a first aid kit, miscellaneous supplies, and a few changes of clothing for him and Lilith to another backpack. They had instructed Luke and Mary to pack the night before and Lilith ran up to the second floor and grabbed their packs before taking a last sweep of the bedrooms.

"Okay, we're both done." Luke stood up.

"Very good." Rufus got up and gathered the maps. Everyone watched as he set them in the sink, struck a match and threw it onto the only evidence of their escape route.

"What the fuck?" Luke ran into the kitchen, but Rufus stopped him as he was trying to turn on the water. "Let go of me. We need them."

"You do not. You memorized them. No one else should know the route we are about to embark on."

Mary placed her hand on his shoulder. "We got this."

She was right, he could feel it deep in the pit of his stomach. It was like a little ball of energy, lighting the way to his mind's library. The route was stored there, all he had to do was take it off the shelf. He closed his eyes and the pictures unfolded. Through every winding tunnel to the end, he knew it all.

Rufus grabbed the satchel that the maps were kept in and threw it over his shoulder. "There are a few supplies that Octavio and I need to acquire. We will be back shortly. Lilith, please have everything ready for when we return."

Lilith tilted her head and gave a nod of agreement.

After the Guardians left, Mary leaned her elbows on the counter propping her chin on her hands.

"Does anyone feel like telling me what happened to Luke?"

"Okay, it was both awesome and sickening at the same time." Luke paced in the kitchen.

"What are you talking about?" asked Mary.

"It was so weird. I was upstairs in the bathroom. I felt woozy, so I sat down and when I looked up, I saw two men, like a hologram. Their voices were jumbled. I started to focus on them and heard Lilith's voice, so I figured they were here in the house. When I thought about the living room—I was there. Or at least my mind was. This is by far the weirdest—and coolest—thing I've ever done."

Mary raised a brow and then sarcastically blurted out, "Even weirder than wings? Sorry, I know this is big. I'm just so damn frustrated. I wish they'd just let me have mine already—or deny me."

"Enough," Lilith abruptly interrupted. "This isn't some high school competition. Literally *everything* is at stake. We need to be focused and sharp. No time for self-pity. Got it?"

Mary nodded in agreement and sat down on the floor, her back against the couch.

Luke slid down beside her. "So how come you were the only one to see me, Lilith?"

"Because you are connected to Mary, and she is connected to me. Unfortunately, that means Araqiel will be able to see you, too. You should be able to learn to control this, so you can appear to whomever you choose—or remain unseen. It's like a light switch. You can turn it off and on except when there is a strong, binding connection like you have with Mary. She will always be able to see you. You should start practicing. Start with small distances, then work up to greater ones."

"Will I be able to go and see my family?"

"Eventually, yes. But that'll take practice. There will come a time, however, that there will be no boundaries to the distance you will be able to go."

"Cool." Luke tightened his fingers and curling them in, motioned to Mary to make a fist bump. She returned the gesture.

"I have to admit, that *is* cool." Mary's words were genuine, confirmed by her Duchenne smile.

"Samael and I want to be clear with you both. This is going to be long and very dangerous. The tunnels will afford us a certain amount of coverage, but they are not cloaked like these hills are; it's too large to do that. Be cautious, stay aware and stay smart at all times. Listen to Octavio and Rufus when they tell you to do something. It literally could be what saves your life. Samael and I will be with you, but if it comes to a choice of staying with the Guardians or us, you stay with them. Do you understand?"

"What do you mean if we have to choose? Why would we have to do that?" Mary's voice trembled.

"The most important thing is that you reach Michael. There may come a time where we are faced with the enemy and the only way out is to separate. If that happens, you stay with the Guardians. Am I clear?"

"Yes." Mary turned her cheek.

Lilith reached her hand out to her daughter. Gently, she took it into hers and caressed the back, outlining the tiny bones. "I love you, my girl. Your safety is everything to me. Please heed what I say."

Mary reluctantly agreed. "Promise me, though, that we will do everything to try and stay together."

The corners of Lilith's mouth curved up and her eyes softened. "I promise that letting you go will not be my option."

"Okay." Mary knew what her mom had implied. When it happens, when she's taken, Lilith would have to abide.

Luke stretched and then stood up. "Let's roll." He turned to Mary. "You ready?"

"I am." She grabbed her pack and strapped it on.

They made one last scan of the house and then single file stepped through the doorway to the outside world, and the precipice of the unknown.

The Guardians had a car waiting about half a mile down the road. They would drive to the opening of the first tunnel and then be on foot the rest of the way.

The tunnels were hidden in a remote hillside behind the development. The silence in the car was foreplay for the brewing tension, Luke kept tapping his thigh with his fingers and Mary was snapping and unsnapping one of the pockets on her cargo pants. Lilith turned around from the front seat and was about to say something when Samael discreetly shook his head in a no motion. She turned back toward the passing scenery.

"I'm proud of the both of you." Samael leaned forward to see Luke and Mary evenly. "You've had a lot of crap happen in a short time. It's not easy for anyone your age, but to literally carry the fate of the world on your shoulders is a complete shit storm."

Luke chortled. "Did you just say, 'shit storm'?"

Lilith chimed in. "Yes, Samael can be quite colorful at times."

"I'm serious. This is more than anyone your age should have to deal with." Samael sat back and gazed out of the window.

"Well, that may be true, but we're not like other people our age. Or at least most of them." Mary had a little sour tone to her voice.

"Yeah. I think we're past the adulation. Fighting to save our lives and those of everyone we love is something anyone our age would do if faced with the challenge," said Luke.

"But that's just it." Samael leaned forward again. "They don't have to and never will. Who you are defined your *place* in this war, but it didn't give you the *courage*. Especially you, Mary. You could have chosen differently."

"Still could." Mary's sour note turned into sarcasm.

"I don't believe that. No matter what your father thinks." Samael reached pass Luke and put his hand on Mary's shoulder. "I think you will fight for heaven and earth, with every ounce of strength that you possess."

"Can you be so sure?" Mary muttered.

"I have faith in you." Samael pulled back. "And I'm never wrong."

Lilith looked back at Samael and rolled her eyes. "Did I ever mention that Samael is an extremely humble angel?"

Luke looked over at Mary and she reluctantly grinned.

When they arrived at the end of the paved road, Octavio, who was driving, pulled over.

"Everyone please exit the vehicle. Rufus, you remain with them until I return."

"Of course."

"What's he doing?" asked Luke.

"It would be better to not leave the vehicle in the open."

Octavio drove the car down to the edge of an embankment. Popping it into neutral, he stepped out. From the rear of the car, he pushed with both arms extended, hands planted on the trunk. The iron horse disappeared down the slope, bumping its way through the brush until it rested in a thick cluster of wax myrtle and southern California pine. He waved his arm indicating for them to follow him.

Rufus took up the rear, Samael right in front of him. Lilith positioned herself behind Octavio, leaving Luke and Mary sandwiched between all of them. They paraded to a dead end of hillside. Octavio tapped the rock in various places before retrieving a piece of white chalk from his pocket. Drawing a doorway on the surface of the stone, he stood back. Extending his arms up to the heavens, he recited, "Όταν βρείτε Ότ μέρος που αναζητάτε, σημειώστε Ότ σημείο που θέλετε να κοιτάξετε."

Luke bent his head behind Samael's ear and whispered, "That sounds different than the Hebrew you used to open the angel doorway."

"That's because it's Greek."

"Oh. What's it mean?"

"It doesn't translate the same, but basically he said, *when you find the place you are looking for, mark the place you want to look.*"

Abruptly, the earth parted, revealing a darkened passageway.

Twenty feet in, a spiral staircase descended into blackness. Bright light cut through the dark as Octavio and Rufus switched on a pair of LED flashlights. The steps were narrow and steep, which made their descent gradual at best. The air thickened with humidity and the passage grew hotter the lower they went. Luke swiped his forearm across his forehead. He rested for a moment in hopes it would cool him off a little. Glancing to Mary above him, beads of sweat from her upper lip had trickled down onto her chin. She wiped it off with her hand and then on her pant leg.

"You okay?" he asked.

"Yeah. You?"

"Livin' the dream." He rubbed the back of his neck. "Octavio, how far down does the staircase go?"

"About half a mile. But some of the journey we'll go deeper."

Luke pressed his anxiety into the iron railing, claustrophobia had bothered him ever since he'd been accidently locked in a closet during a game of hide and seek when he was six. The idea of being so far underground heightened his fear of separation from everything and everyone he loved. He'd get through it, but not without the shadows of trauma that followed him.

"How deep do you think we've gone so far?" Luke's mouth felt dry.

"We've got about another twenty minutes to go before we reach bottom. You okay?"

"Oh yeah. Just curious." Luke hoped he'd sounded confident.

Lilith rang out. "Mary, how are you doing?"

"I'm good. Just sweaty. It's really hot in here."

"It should get a little better once we're off this staircase. Right, Octavio?"

"Yes, ma'am." Octavio responded.

Lilith couldn't resist. "That's what I love about you, Octavio. You're a man of many words."

Samael, Mary, and Luke enjoyed a laugh at Octavio's expense. Octavio glared over his shoulders, and then resumed the journey.

"This is going to be a long trip," muttered Rufus.

Luke squinted, straining his eyes to get a better view of their surroundings. The beams from the two flashlights were bright, but most of the time they were pointed straight down to light the way for their travel.

He could tell by the feel of his weight on the steps they were more like stone than wood. He brushed his foot across the mass, it was definitely solid. They crackled like wax paper every time their shoes took a step to descend. At first, he thought it might be moisture but a passing illumination from Octavio's flashlight revealed a grainy dust coating on most of the stone. Luke dropped his gaze to get a closer look. The rough layer was actually pieces of the masonry that had broken off and crushed over time. Revealing jagged edges and large cracks atop the patina, he kept his hand on the wall to avoid dominoing his way to the bottom.

His fingers followed the lines of the structure, the oblong shapes separated by a seam of rough gravel-like substance suggested they were bricks. Cooler than the air surrounding them, a fair amount of heat resonated from the surface reminding him of the oven they descended to. As his hands glided over the finish, he noticed a pattern etched into the mass of masonry.

He turned back to Rufus. "Is there writing on the walls?"

Rufus nodded his head.

"Care to elaborate?" Luke wasn't giving up so easily.

Octavio chimed in. "They're incantations used to keep a

barrier between the travelers of the tunnels and anyone or anything that would interrupt their journey."

"So—any evil things? Is that what you're trying to say? It's to protect us from Lucifer's army? That's great."

"Not really." Octavio sounded like a drone spewing out facts.

"Why? How is that not great?" Luke was perplexed.

"Because over the years, some of the walls have cracked from earthquakes and ground settling. The incantations have been disrupted, leaving them virtually useless in some parts of the tunnels."

"Well, aren't you a beacon of hope."

"You are the one that asked, my young friend. Do not blame me for what happened. When these tunnels were built, they didn't take the shifting of the earth into consideration. They did remarkable work for the tools they had to work with. It took them two centennials to construct them. Many men died working down here. My father was one of them. There are enough of the words to help us. Be thankful."

Luke felt foolish. He had no idea of Octavio's connection to the tunnels. How could he? Yet he still felt like a horse's ass.

"Sorry, dude. I had no idea."

"He died for what he believed in. I only wish to be as fortunate."

Breaths echoed in the darkness. It didn't seem appropriate to Luke to pursue further conversation. Judging by the singular noise of shoes hitting the steps, everyone agreed. Still straining to see the writing, his mind wandered to what it must have been like for the souls who devoted their lives to its construction. Living most of your days in darkness and knowing the forces of evil were on your heels, made it even creepier. It's one thing to deal with Lucifer's army in the light of day. But down here, secluded and maneuvering through the earth's underbelly with no direction or real light to guide you, must have been beyond challenging.

Octavio was the first to reach solid ground. "We're here at the bottom." His tone as void of emotion as their last conversation.

After stepping down, Luke approached Octavio. "Can I use the flashlight?"

Octavio knitted his brow. "Must you?"

"I wanna get a better look at the walls. I'll be careful."

Hesitantly, Octavio handed it to him. Luke pointed it toward the wall so he could get a better view of the results of years of labor that had gone into the creation of this lifeline. He scanned the beam upward, then downward toward the ground. Every space was amply filled with words and symbols. He quickly spun to his right. The opposing wall looked exactly the same as all the others.

"This is incredible. Is this Hebrew?" He handed the flashlight to Mary and ambled closer. With the tips of his fingers, he traced the lines and crevices as if reading braille.

"Aramaic," said Octavio.

"Whoa, I thought that was a dead language."

"Not dead . . . forgotten."

"Is there anything we can say, like a spell or something to protect us when the carvings are worn off?"

"No. I'm sorry. It's been tried in the past, only to fail."

Luke swiped his brow. *It seems stupid, not to have a back-up plan.*

"The walls look identical, Octavio. Is there a reason?" Mary's eye darted from side to side.

"Yes." Octavio reached for the flashlight.

"And?" Luke huffed.

"It stops the invader from returning to the surface the same way from which they came."

Luke took a moment to think about what he had just said. He glanced over to Mary. Her face looked as perplexed as he felt.

"Wait. Are you saying they can't go back up? That means we can't either."

"That is exactly what it means." Octavio started walking away.

"How the shit does that make any sense? I thought the words were to keep them from penetrating the tunnels, not trap them here." Luke surged toward the spiral staircase. He put one foot forward and tried to step up. He was instantly thrown back and landed on his ass. Mary scrambled over to him, but he was quickly back on his feet. She made a go at it and wound up on her bottom, too.

"You can try as many times as you like, but you are not getting topside that way. It was to stop the demons from alerting others. Should one of them unwittingly find their way in the tunnels, the Guardians can dispose of them and their legions would be none the wiser."

"So, you've basically sandwiched us in between Heaven and Hell." Luke was pissed off.

"You are nowhere near either place." Octavio sounded genuinely confused.

"We're on our way to Michael." Luke pointed in the direction they were headed. "So, that's Heaven. Behind us . . ." Again, Luke pointed, but this time in the direction they had come. "Lucifer's goons can potentially hunt us down. So, that's Hell. And us?" Luke patted himself on the chest. "We're the meat that holds this sandwich together, and someone just might take a bite."

Octavio's eyebrows knitted together. "Why do you keep making references to a sandwich? Are you hungry?"

Luke was too overcome with humor to remain angry. "Never mind. Lead the way." Luke extended his arm and bowed at the waist.

"Stay close together," Octavio instructed.

Mary winced. "Luke," Mary whispered. "I think I hurt my ankle back there. It's throbbing."

"Is it bad?"

"It really hurts. Can you get Lilith?"

"Sure."

Luke hopped to the back of the procession to alert Lilith. She immediately went to her daughter.

"Okay, let's sit and I'll take a look."

"Uhhh, can I help you?" Luke fumbled with his hands in the air not knowing where to grab her.

"Thanks." Mary clutched his arm and he hesitantly glided it around her waist and eased her to the ground.

Carefully removing her sneaker and sock Lilith pressed gently. Not feeling any signs of a broken bone, she elevated the foot on her bent knee. "Mary's going to need a little time to relieve pressure off this ankle. Why don't you all go on ahead and we'll catch up."

Samael was the first to interject. "No one is separating. If we have to wait, then so be it. We stay together."

Luke nodded his head adamantly in agreement.

"Nonsense." Everyone turned their attentions to Octavio. "Just heal her." He peered over to Luke.

"What the hell you looking at me for? I don't know how to heal anything."

"Of course, you do. It's one of your powers. The best one if you ask me."

"You don't know much I wish I had that one right now, but I don't. Wait, do you know which ones I get?"

"I do. Please don't ask me to reveal them. The celestials think it's best to receive one at a time without distraction or impatience."

"But . . ."

Octavio put his hand up, then averted his attention to Lilith.

"I had hoped we would be further along by now."

"No. The astral projection is only the second ability to materialize." Lilith was gently massaging Mary's ankle.

"Which was the first?" Octavio questioned.

"He can slow his heartbeat." Lilith was still concentrating on Mary while Octavio huffed and turned away.

Mary winced as she turned her ankle back and forth trying to stretch out the muscles.

"Here, put your leg in my lap and I'll massage your ankle. That might work better than stretching it," said Lilith.

"Okay."

As Lilith turned to get into position, her hair fell to the side revealing the full picture of the tattoo on her back—a snake tightly wrapped around an open hand. Mary quickly retracted and pressed her body into the wall.

"Mary, what's wrong?" Lilith's eyes widened.

"Get away from me, you're one of them." Mary screeched.

"What's going on?" Luke raised his voice.

"Lilith is a servant of Lucifer. She has the mark Michael told us about. It's on her back."

Luke jumped to his feet. "Let me see."

"It's not what you think. I have the tattoo, yes. But I have never served the Dark Prince."

Luke grabbed the neck of her t-shirt and yanked, revealing the serpent.

"Hands off." Samael intervened. "Lilith bears the mark because Araqiel branded her when he first took her. It's a tactic to break down your prisoner, but it didn't work. She's too strong to ever give in."

"How come you still have it?" Mary mumbled.

"It's a reminder of how hateful your father truly is. I used it to get me through all the years I was looking for you. One day, I'll have it removed. Today's not that day."

"I'm sorry. It just scared me."

Lilith gently massaged her daughter's ankle. "I get it. I should have told you. There's so much we'll need to talk about when this is all over. For now though, let's see if we can make you feel better." Lilith smiled.

Samael was standing beside Rufus when he noticed a flicker of light coming from behind them. He grabbed the flashlight from Rufus and pointed down the tunnel—nothing. The light that flashed across the darkness a moment ago had disappeared. He calmed his breathing and honed his hearing.

"Samael, I hear something," Luke whispered.

"Yes, so do . . . Run! They're here!"

Samael scooped up Mary and threw her on his back. "Go!"

Luke ran mindlessly into the tunnel system. Lilith turned and grabbed his upper arm, flinging him in front of her. He didn't argue. The tunnels grew darker the further they went, and navigation became treacherous. Memorizing the map was useless if you couldn't see five feet in front of you.

"We need a plan. This is not gonna work." Luke slowed down.

"Luke. What the hell? Get your ass going." Lilith's voice commanded.

"No. How long do you think Samael can keep this up?"

"You're right. We need to stop them." Lilith slid a mallet from her belt.

"Okay, not exactly what I had in mind, but that will work, too."

"Samael, wait," she called out.

He stopped and turned around, leaning his shoulder into the rock for relief.

The group quickly caught up to them.

"What if we hide Mary, and then meet them head on?"

"I'm going with all of you. My ankle is sore, but my fists work just fine." Mary let go of Samael and slid down to the ground. Gently, she placed her foot down and walked around. "It's getting better. What's the plan?"

"Whatever it is, we better execute quickly. They're getting close." Samael pulled a large knife from the back of his jeans.

Octavio cleared his throat like he was about to give The Gettysburg Address. "If we keep going, we will be fine. The spells are in good condition deeper in. We just have to go another one hundred feet or so and they will be trapped. Eventually they'll die."

"I get they're trapped but are you sure they'll die? They're demons."

"I don't think they are. They're probably humans who have been conditioned." Octavio peered down the dark tunnel.

"Conditioned? What does that mean?"

"I'll explain later. We're running out of time." Octavio swiftly turned and positioned himself in the back with Rufus. Samael grabbed Mary, but she insisted on running on her own. Luke was about to take her hand and make a dash, when a deep, resonating growl filled the space around them. The reverberation nearly knocked them off their feet.

"Human? Sure, whatever you say." Luke gripped Mary's hand. "We need to go now." He was pulling her forward when he heard a blood curdling scream.

Luke looked on in horror as a large, disfigured, human-like creature scaled the wall and took Mary in his grip. Its long fingers wrapped around her waist and yanked. Mary's limp body flew to the creature. It cinched her close, before escaping down an alternate tunnel. Luke tried to push through Lilith and the others, but they were busy fighting off two more of the humanesque fiends. Whatever happened to them had given them inhuman strength. One tossed Samael and Octavio like they were plastic dolls. The other had a firm grip on Lilith's hair as Rufus attacked him with blow after insignificant blow. Luke abruptly looked up at the tunnel ceiling and then back at the menagerie of war.

Lilith screamed, "Go!"

Luke stepped into the middle of the tunnel and concentrated. He wriggled as the flesh of his back began to stretch apart. Again, he focused—willing his body to comply. He plastered his arms at his side, ignoring the pain forging through his shoulders. He hadn't completely healed yet, but time wasn't a luxury he could afford. The wind rose up, swooshing around him, lifting him upward. Thrusting forward, his limbs stiffened to harness the surge pumping through his veins. His heart crushed against his rib cage as torrents of blood flooded the chambers. He rose until he was clear of any interference. Rumbling echoed down the chamber and shook the stone walls as he shot past his friends. With his wings at half extension to maneuver through the tunnel, rage guided his thoughts. For the first time in seven months, he knew he was capable of murder. It didn't matter to him that Mary's captor is human, or rather, was human. Whatever it was now, he had no problem ripping its head from its neck. Everything was happening so fast, and yet his mind could process with no problem. He could formulate and categorize everything in his brain. Priority—get Mary, then kill the thing. Help the others, and finally resume their journey. It was all very clear and precise. Hate was a tool he'd use to take that thing's life, and he was okay with it.

Mary's screams drew Luke further away from the others. The walls of the passage were severely damaged, and he feared the worst. If it kept up like this, there was no telling how far he would be led away from everyone.

Flying in the darkness came with its own challenges. Luke tried to keep his mind clear and be aware of his surroundings, but the walls came at him with every twist and turn. He needed light.

Misjudging the next curve, he clipped the wall with his left wing. Startled, he plummeted to the ground and slammed on the hard surface of compacted dirt. Without checking for injury, he stammered to his feet and took flight again. His mind wandered and centered in on the light he saw just before he received his wings. It was brilliant, almost blinding in the sky. Luke's heartbeat slowed, his breath calmed to a Zen like flow. He was soaring with the skill of an experienced pilot. His fingertips heated like they were passing over a flame, but he ignored it. The writing on the walls was becoming clearer. He surveyed the tunnel as it lit up like someone had just plugged in a thousand Christmas lights. The walls twinkled with the reflection of the warm white glow.

The luminous energy was emanating from his hands. Excitement bubbled up squelching any semblance of calm from moments ago—another power.

Luke took full advantage of his newfound gift. He let his wings spread to full capacity, decreasing the distance between him and Mary much quicker than before. Being able to see where he was going and what new wall was around the next bend gave him the advantage he needed. He would be able to see exactly what he was dealing with. He already knew the strength it possessed. The erratic trail he was taking indicated it had more brawn than brains. And although it was quick, it moved with the grace and balance of an ogre with one leg. Luke could outmaneuver the thing.

Mary's screams grew louder as he closed in. He slowed to get a fix on her. As he hovered in midair, he folded his wings closer to his body to quiet the wind. He sharpened his hearing and focused his thoughts to follow Mary's sounds. After a few moments, he had her. He could almost feel her next to him. He was gliding now, impulsively drawn to her.

He caught up with them just in time to see her punching and kicking to break free from the creature's unyielding grasp.

Tears streamed down her cheeks; her skin grey as she labored to fill her lungs with air. Luke had a clear view of the beast. The hump on its back seemed to press into the spine with such force that it pushed its chest out like a barrel protruding from the neck down toward its belly. Its face badly contorted with a drooping eye, crooked mouth and nose pushed to the left side of its face. The creature's hands and feet were oversized and swelled up like a puffer fish, but surprisingly it did nothing to affect its grip. Its rotund fingers were locked onto Mary and weren't releasing. Wild eyes and barely recognizable words spewed from its mouth.

Luke called out to Mary, and she turned in his direction. The abomination squeezed its grip on her tighter, before heading toward him like the bull to a matador. The beast took a leap, expecting to pounce on its prey, but Luke darted swiftly out of its path, and it slammed into the wall and bounced to the ground. Dazed, it loosened its hold for millisecond, long enough however, for Mary to roll away.

"Mary, get up! Run!" Luke shouted, his voice deepened, echoing through the chamber. Mary stammered to her feet. Eyes wide she looked down at the struggling crazed human, and then back to Luke. Fear was replaced by confusion and frustration, but Luke didn't have time to explain.

"Get out of here. I'll catch up. Quickly, before it's got full senses."

"No. I won't leave you."

"Go, please."

"Which way?"

Luke pointed back toward the tunnel to his right and Mary stumbled, using the walls to guide her way.

He scanned the passage for anything he could use to slow the beast, the fowl creature had gotten to his feet and had his nose in the air. It locked in on her scent and its disfigured body tensed, clenching his puffy hands. The creature spun and stopped in front of the entrance Mary had gone down just moments ago.

She was injured and dazed, she wouldn't get very far before it caught up with her.

Luke lifted his hands to cast light below, then lowered himself until his feet touched the ground. The creature locked in on him and took a step forward but stopped. It spun around and stared down the tunnel then back towards Luke. Something or someone was controlling it. Like a puppet on strings, it resisted as it was forced in Mary's direction. The creature struggled as Luke stretched into the depths of his own power. He leaned against the wall and pushed forward with his soul, leaving his body behind. If he could cloak himself, he might have a better chance of defeating the abomination.

A glint of light caught Luke's eye. On the ground was a knife the creature must have dropped. He glared at it, willing it to come to his hand—nothing. Stammering, the creature no longer resisted the unknown puppeteer. Grunting like a wild beast going after its dinner, it relented, following Mary's scent. Luke was out of time. He needed to make this happen—now. Embracing his angel self, he banked on it superseding his human rationale. If he believed it was happening, then maybe that would be enough for it to work. He hastily walked toward the knife, bent down, and tried again. It still lay on the ground. Over his shoulder, the creature was disappearing down the tunnel. A surge of rage and desperation fueled his core, without a thought he reached down and snatched the blade.

The light emanating from his ghostly hands fixated on the beast who was now swiftly navigating through the tunnel. Luke reached him with the full force of the wind flowing through his majestic wings. He rammed himself into its back and held on with both arms. The blow threw them both to the ground. Luke quickly jumped up and jabbed the knife into the creature's back, slicing up to its neck. A chilling scream pierced Luke's ears, echoing through the barren tunnel. He released his grip on blade and the creature collapsed, spilling to the ground, landing with its face in the dirt.

He looked around for Mary. She was standing in the shadows, exhausted.

"We have to go. I disabled that thing for now. But I don't think it will be long before its back."

She reached out and sliced her hand through his ghostly form. Her hand shaky, she stepped back.

"I thought it might come in handy to kill that thing. I gotta get back to my body, it's this way." Luke pointed. "Can you walk?"

"Yeah, I'm okay."

Luke hovered next to Mary moving along at her pace. Luckily, his body wasn't far off. Still leaning against the stone wall where he left it, Mary got close to his resting shell. She tilted her head to the side examining it closely. "Can you feel anything?" She brushed her fingers across his forearm.

"A little." Luke floated forward and paired his soul with his body.

"Did you see his eyes? Completely void. That poor man was just like us and then some demon like my dad decides his life isn't important. Turns him into—that."

"It was like something is pulling its strings. We're like sitting ducks down here."

"We have to get back to the others."

"I can fly us. It'll be quicker."

"Okay."

He took her hand and pulled her close. Mary awkwardly placed her arms around his neck, and then, scooping her up, Luke took flight through the tunnel.

Flying was easier now. Luke's strength had increased, he could hold Mary with the right arm while lighting the way with his left. Racing back toward the others, Luke was reassured that with his newfound powers of illumination and speed, they would find them quickly.

Mary tightened her grip and nestled her cheek to the crook of his neck. She tried to remain as still as she could to avoid upsetting his balance. When they reached the part of the tunnels where the battle had begun, it was empty. Luke slowed hovering for a moment before easing back to the ground and releasing Mary.

"Are you sure this is where we left them?"

"I'm positive. I can still feel their presence. Try to clear your mind and see if you can, too."

Mary relaxed and closed her lids. She shook her arms until they hung limp at her sides then, lowered her chin to her chest. Moments passed and her head arced to the left. "I can feel them. They were right here in the same spot." A tear trickled from the corner of her eye. "Something bad happened. I know it."

"Me, too. I can't see it, though." Luke clasped her hand and squeezed.

"Me either."

"In my mind, I see a ribbon of colors going that way." He pointed to the tunnel on his right. "I think that's traces of them."

"I don't see it. But if you're right it's the only thing we have to go—"

Suddenly, Mary was thrust forward to the other side of the tunnel, her body hit the wall like a rag doll.

"Mary!"

Luke spun around and was face to face with one of the ogre humans, its arm arced in the air as if it were getting ready to release the same force on him. Luke grabbed the creature's forearm with both of his hands and locked his grip. He picked the ogre up and beat it against the wall several times. The creature squealed with pain, and after letting out a few grunts, lay lifeless in a pool of blood. Its broken body making it more unrecognizable as a human. For a moment, Luke felt sorry for the battered creature. It once had a life, perhaps a family and friends. But when he saw Mary lying crumpled and motionless, his compassion quickly faded.

Luke rushed to her side, his insides trembling with fear. He knelt down and raised her limp body into his arms. He listened to her chest for signs of life, detecting a faint beat like a clock winding down from failing batteries. The once-pink hue in her cheeks was grey and her flesh cool to the touch. He held her tight against his chest, trying to will the warmth back into her veins.

"Mary," he whispered softly in her ear. "Please don't leave me. I can't do this without you—I don't want to." He stood up and lifted her to her feet. Holding her firmly against his chest, he released his wings and folded them around their bodies. Like a cocoon, they nestled together in the warmth of Luke's energy.

"Breathe. Feel my strength. Use it to come back to me."

He lowered his head and pressed it up against hers. He listened for breath but heard nothing. Pulling her even closer, he felt the passing beats of her slowing heart.

"No. Mary, you listen to my voice. You follow it back to me. You are not going anywhere. Do you hear me?" Luke's mind raced. Heat rose from his pit spreading along the highway of veins and muscles. His face glowed with the intensity of flames from a torch. Hot air flowed beneath them, lifting the young lovers up and suspending them midair. Luke closed his wings tighter and concentrated on Mary's heart. He envisioned it beating steadily and strong, and then spreading to repair any damage that was taking her away. He imagined bones that were broken, healing and becoming whole. Torn muscles fusing together and lungs easily expanding then releasing. He forced all his energy into reviving her dying body.

Completely drained, the heat dissipated as quickly as it had arisen. They dropped to the ground, still encased in Luke's wings. He was exhausted and could barely move. Slowly, he unfurled from the feathery protection and Mary rolled onto her side facing the wall. Luke gazed at her lifeless body and sobbed. He had failed. His love was now lost to him forever. Lying down beside her, he put his arm over her and pulled her close.

"What . . . what happened?"

"Mary!" Luke gently rolled her towards him. "I thought I'd lost you."

"I heard you calling me and then it got really hot. It felt like my body was about to burst into flames. After that, I could breathe again."

"You were almost dead. Your heart was barely beating. I—brought you back, healed you." He wiped the tears out of his eyes and off his cheeks.

"You've got it. The healing power."

Mary put her hand on his cheek, she leaned in capturing his lips. Luke trembled, tracing the lines of her face with his fingertips, he gave in to his long burning desire. The yearning to explore her body and give himself completely to her would be so easy to do. Toss aside the prophecy, just be teenagers. But the flash of the broken corpse of a thing that once had desires of their own, stole his moment of pleasure.

Pulling back, he gently brushed the hair away from her face and whispered, "Time to go."

He got up and put his hand out, she laid her palm into his and squeezed. He lifted her up. They exchanged a moment of longing with their eyes before he reeled back to reality.

"We have to find the others. They're in danger." Luke stood looking down the tunnel. The ribbon of colors had started to fade. "We need to do something fast; their trail is beginning to dissipate."

"It might be quicker if you travel out of body."

"I'm not leaving you." His stance stiffened.

"I'll be fine. You killed that thing. I'll wait here with your body. As soon as you know where they are, you can come back for me."

"I nearly lost you. I'm not taking that risk again."

"What if we're about to lose them? Can you live with knowing you could have prevented it? I can't." Mary looked pleadingly into his eyes.

She was right. It would be quicker for him to go and look for them in spirit, but he couldn't shake the feeling of doom when he thought about leaving her.

"I'll find them and be right back for you. I have no light to give you."

"It'll be okay. I have the memory of our kiss to light the way." She rolled her eyes.

"Oh, you didn't just say that." He ran his hand down her arm and laced her fingers with his. "I'm serious, though, just stay put. Do not go anywhere."

"I won't. Go. Find them." She pushed him away.

Letting his head drop, it was but a moment before he was standing by Mary's side.

"I'm not sure I can get used to this." Mary's gaze bounced from celestial to Luke's slumped body.

"I'm starting to like this power." He winked at her and floated away toward the fading lines of color. He looked back and lit the way to see Mary one more time. She was sitting next to his body. He waved to her, and she blew him a kiss. Then darkness filled the tunnel behind him.

SEVEN

Luke took comfort in the beating of Mary's heart. He wasn't sure if it was his hearing that was becoming more astute or the fact that his corporeal being lay close to her. Their connection was strong. Either way, he was happy he could still have some assurance that she was okay.

It was strange to be traveling so far from his body. He doubted this was the best plan, but it had made sense a few minutes ago. He was able to travel swiftly. He concentrated on Lilith and Samael, their images strong in his mind. An invisible rope pulled at him, guiding him down the passages of the unending tunnel.

He followed as the ribbon grew thicker and more brilliant, certain he was getting close. Still, a part of him feared the unknown. He had no idea if the colors were leading him to life or death. His new powers were an asset but not knowing how to fully use and understand them was daunting.

He heard voices and stopped short. They were faint, far away. It was Lilith. She was barely audible. *Was she whispering?*

"Luke. Luke, are you there?" Her voice sounded small, like she was a million miles away. "I can feel you. You're near. Be careful, there are four of them. They have us chained and they're waiting for you."

"Lilith, can you hear me?" His words resonated through the air carried purely by the will of his thoughts. "I won't let them see me."

"Be very careful. They are unusually strong." Luke focused in on the sound of Lilith's voice, blocking out any unwanted distractions. He moved quickly, flowing to Lilith like a magnet. The closer he got to her and the others the more intense the energy streaming through him became.

"Stop. You're very close. Come in slowly and see if you can unlock these chains. The key is dangling from the pocket of the one in grey. He seems to be a little more intelligent than the rest, which isn't saying much. Their strength is the only way they were able to trap us."

Luke focused once again and found himself standing beside the bound Lilith. Samael was slumped over next to her, Octavio and Rufus lay bloodied and bruised on the floor on the other side of the cave. Luke locked eyes with Lilith who tilted her head towards the ogre in grey. He saw the sparkle of metal bouncing off from the light of the lantern beside it. He crept through the gang of demonic puppets until he was standing in front of the target ogre.

The distorted face looked right into his eyes and didn't even know it. Luke pivoted around its side and gently reached for the key, but he swiped through it like the ghostly manifestation he was. Just like earlier with the knife, he had to concentrate.

He glanced over at Lilith. She locked eyes with him and reassuringly nodded her head in encouragement. He hesitated for a moment and then using his mind to see his hand grabbing the key, he reached again. This time he felt it. Cautiously he lifted the key away from the beast's pocket, securing it in his fist. The ogre human turned up his nose and sniffed. Luke stopped —frozen. Sniffing once more, the beast turned its' head side to side assessing the dimly lit tunnel. A few moments passed and then, seemingly satisfied, he relaxed. Luke swiftly moved behind Lilith and unlocked her chains.

One by one he went to the others and released them. Samael was the only one not to move after he was free. Luke searched the area for anything they could use as weapons. They needed help. If those things were strong enough to subdue an ancient angel like Samael, overcoming them wasn't going to be easy. He noticed a sheath hanging from the belt of two of the beasts. The other two didn't seem to be armed.

Using their telepathic connection, he communicated his plan to Lilith.

I'm going after the blades.

Be careful, that one in the middle seems exceptionally strong. He was the one who got to Samael.

Swiftly he rose and circled the four beasts picking up speed as he circled around them. Concentrating on each of the knives, he reached out grabbing the first one and yanking it free. The beast spun around searching for who had taken his weapon. Seeing nobody, he let out a loud screech. The other three stood up straight with fists folded and ready to fight. Luke raced to snag the remaining blade, pulling it free. He threw a knife to Lilith and one to Rufus then, as a distraction, stood in the center of the tunnel and materialized. The beasts lunged for him, missing their ghostly target, they slammed into one another, crash landing on the cavern floor. Luke shot toward the ceiling and hovered above them.

Letting out a loud roar, they swatted at him. Their twisted, thick arms carved through Luke, and they grew frustrated, ignoring their prisoners.

With a precise movement tunt both Lilith and Rufus snuck behind the creatures. They nodded once in cue then each cupped the chin of a beast, drawing the blades across the thick flesh of its' neck, releasing a rush of bright, warm blood. The beasts grabbed their throats and collapsed to the ground. When the remaining two realized what was happening, they lunged for Lilith and Rufus.

Lilith plunged her knife into the side of the ogre human who had her in its grip. Yelping in pain it let go and Lilith fell to the dirt. Scrambling to get back up she lunged at it again and this time pierced the knife through its chest penetrating the heart. It fell to the ground with a prominent thud.

Rufus wasn't as lucky. His opponent, the one Lilith had warned Luke about, was equally as dense as his other cohorts, but possessed the strength of ten men. He picked Rufus up with ease and slammed him into a tunnel wall. Rufus's motionless frame slithered to the ground.

The beast turned to Lilith, but Octavio came from behind and, with both fists clenched, sent a powerful punch into its left kidney. Spinning around it went for Octavio with all its power. Wrapping its enormous forearm around his throat, it drained the air from the man's lungs.

Luke reached for the knife that was sticking out of the dead beast but once again, his hand flowed right through it. Lilith scrambled to the body and gripped the knife in both hands, wrenching it from the lifeless chest. Lilith struggled to her feet and with every ounce of energy she had, plunged the knife into the beast's throat. It slid into the flesh, severing the jugular. Octavio dropped to the ground, coughing as the beast clutched its' throat and collapsed.

"Where's Mary?"

"She's with my body. I can hear her heartbeat, she's okay."

Moaning, Rufus's lids fluttered as he stretched his limbs. Lilith curled up by Samael's side, he lay unconscious.

"What happened to him?" Luke was standing over the both of them.

"That thing overpowered him and used a small metal tip on

its' finger to scratch him. My guess is it was laced with some kind of poison. See if you can find it."

Luke let the light flow through his hands lighting up the tunnel like the rising sun. First, he checked the fingers of all the deceased beasts—nothing. He then rose toward the ceiling of the tunnel and scoured the dirt below. Nestled close to one of the walls something glittered, catching his eye. Floating down he reached out and grabbed a small metal piece that resembled a pointed thimble, he set it Lilith's palm.

She brought it up to her nose and smelled. "Definitely poison."

"Octavio, do you recognize this scent? It's very sweet."

Octavio grabbed the small metal and waved it under his nose.

"I do know what this is, but I haven't come across it in years. I'm afraid Samael has been poisoned with Cerbera Odollom."

"What? How is that possible? You can't even get that in the states."

"Lilith. You know better than anyone what Araqiel is capable of. If he wants it—he gets it."

"Oh, God. What are we gonna do?" Lilith swiped her eyes.

"I can try to heal him." Luke folded down beside Samael.

"You haven't acquired that power yet." Octavio knitted his brow.

"I saved Mary. She was dying. Broken bones, torn insides and somehow it just kicked in."

"Well, that's good news, however it won't help us."

"Why?" asked Luke.

"Because the art of healing with poison is very different than broken bones. I'm afraid we'll need a good old-fashioned anecdote to help Samael."

"He's an angel. That's the only reason he's still alive." They all turned to Rufus who was now struggling to his feet. "His body is not human, so I think remaining unconscious is its' way of fighting back. We need to get the cure. His heart is slowing. Soon it will stop.”

“But how?” Lilith kissed her love. “Where can I get it?”

Luke wondered how she could go from emotional to warrior in seconds.

“Because his life depends on it.” She huffed.

“How the . . .?” Luke stopped himself.

“Out of body power. If you direct your thoughts toward someone, they’ll hear you.”

Lilith walked over to Rufus and glared into his eyes. “Where?”

“I know someone who can help. But you’re going to have to go alone and retrieve it. Luckily, he isn’t too far from here. A little further north. I’ll give you his information and tell him I sent you. But be swift, we don’t have much time. Clearly, they know where we are. Tell him you need Digibind to cure a broken heart. He’ll know what you mean.”

“Wait.” Luke interjected. “How is she getting out? She can’t go back and there’s no exit until we reach Michael.”

“There’s no exit that you can see.” Rufus interjected.

“What do you mean?” Luke spun around to Octavio. “What is he talking about?”

“I can create an exit for Lilith to leave, but she won’t be able to get back in without me. We must keep going to keep Luke and Mary on the path to Michael. I can open a passage, but when you return, you will have to let me know so I can let you enter.”

“So, what’s the problem?” Luke knitted his brows in frustration.

Lilith let out a loud sigh. “What Octavio is saying is that I’ll have no way to let him know I’m back. All of you will be down here, and I’ll be top side. I won’t know exactly where you are, and I won’t have a way of communicating with you.”

"Octavio, give her the necklace." Rufus pointed to a small brass circle hanging from a chain around his neck.

"I can't. It is Michael's only way of tracking us." Octavio placed his hand over the charm.

"I think Michael will understand. Lilith won't be that long. Once she's back you can open the doorway and Michael will have sights on us again."

"Yes. But you don't understand. He'll think we've all gone topside. He'll assume something has happened."

"Well brother, it has. We don't have any other choice if Lilith is to get back." Rufus put his hand on Octavio's shoulder.

Hesitantly, Octavio took the necklace off and gave it to Lilith. She placed it around her neck and tucked it into her shirt.

"When you arrive at the tunnel, clasp the charm and focus on me. It will let me know you are here. I will open the doorway at this spot so you will be near Samael. Once he is better, clasp it again and it will show you the way to us. If there's a problem, Luke can come to you once you're down below again."

Lilith nodded. "Oh, wait. How will it tell me which way to go?"

"You'll recognize it when it happens." Octavio frowned with impatience. "We really must get to Mary."

"Yes. Go." Lilith bent down and kissed the top of Samael's head. "Okay Octavio, do your thing."

Octavio stood by the wall to the left and chanted. The wall crumbled, sending a cloud of dust in the air. As it settled, a staircase appeared. In moments, she was out of their sight and the staircase gone.

Luke knew Octavio and Rufus could find their way to Mary on their own. But sticking together seemed like a better plan. With him lighting the way, the two Guardians followed closely behind.

A heavy weight pulled at Luke, doubt and regret rushed to

fill the hollow spaces that his confidence had vacated. It was the first day of their journey and they had only encountered six ogres. His strength and abilities should have been enough to overcome them—but they weren't. How could he fulfill a prophecy if he couldn't take care of a few of Lucifer's rejects on his own?

He glanced back at the two guardians. Rufus was limping and Octavio had a huge gash across his forehead. Although they were keeping up with him, it was clear they would have to rest. It wasn't a bad idea . . . Luke was feeling a little dizzy himself.

"Hey, you guys doing okay?" Luke stumbled.

"You're the one who seems to be having an issue." Octavio sped up until he was beside Luke.

"You've been disconnected from your body for quite a while. Are you feeling dizzy or nauseous?"

"A little dizzy. But I'm all right." Luke looked down toward the ground.

"We can stop if you need to rest for a moment." Octavio waved back at Rufus to slow down.

"No. We need to keep going. I'm fine."

"The longer you are away, the more you risk a permanent celestial state."

"What are you talking about? I may not be able to get back into my body?"

"Right now, you're fine. It has been a while but not long enough to have a lasting effect. But . . . yes. You could lose the connection with your body if you remain in this state for too long of a time."

"How long is too long?" Luke grew agitated.

"There's no exact time frame, but you'll know."

Octavio stopped. "If you get so dizzy that you can't stand, will yourself back immediately. If you should be rendered unconscious, you will wake up in this celestial state with no end. Understand?"

"It would have been nice if someone would have mentioned it before."

"Would you have done this differently?"

"No."

"Then I'm telling you now." Octavio resumed walking.

"Why give me this power if it could wind up killing me?"

"Well, you wouldn't be dead." His tone was condescending.

"Octavio, you're pissing me off. Spirit— no body equals dead."

"Not dead. Just not connected. Honestly, Luke, how is this so hard for you to understand? Your blood will still flow, your heart still beat, but your soul will not be there in your body. Your essence, everything that you feel, think, want, that will be corporeal."

"That's fucking worse than death. I'll live forever?"

"Hardly. Your body will still be vulnerable to death. And when that happens, you will transition to the next realm."

Rufus mumble under his breath, "Inexperienced boys leading the way, we're doomed." Luke's astute hearing homed in on every word. He knew he should hold his tongue and not say anything, but he couldn't.

"You know Rufus, it's this inexperienced boy that rescued your ass. I think if you're gonna grumble, you need to start with yourself."

Rufus didn't respond. In fact, both he and Octavio were silent for the rest of the way. Which was good because after hearing the news about this particular power, Luke was not in the mood to further their conversation.

When they reached Mary, she had fallen asleep next to his still figure. Quickly, he willed his spirit back into the security of his outer shell. As soon as he moved, she woke up.

"Oh, thank God you're back. I was getting so worried. What happened? Wait— where's Lilith and Samael?"

Luke explained everything.

"How was Samael when you left?" She scrambled to her feet.

"He was out cold. I'm not sure if he could even hear anything that was going on."

"Maybe you guys shouldn't have left him."

"Well, it turns out, I couldn't have stayed anyway." Luke's tone was sarcastic.

He peered over at Octavio and Rufus while he quickly caught Mary up.

"Okay. What the fuck?" Mary's face glowed with anger. She swiftly turned to the guardians. "You both knew this?"

They shook their heads in agreement.

"He could've died."

Octavio interjected, "Not died, he—."

"Don't!" Luke's voice was commanding.

Mary sat down again with her back against the stone. She extended her arm out for Luke to join her. He slid down the wall and rested his hand in hers and his head on her shoulder. Turning, his cheek brushed the nape of Mary's neck and he wriggled closer. He closed his eyes, hoping Lilith would be back soon.

Eight

Luke wriggled his shoulders, trying to acclimate with his own flesh. It was good to get back to his body, but it left him with lingering tactile confusion. The limitations of blood and bones were easily forgotten when he was celestial. It was a freedom he didn't think he could ever truly describe to someone who hadn't experienced it. A part of him yearned to return to his ghostly being.

"Octavio. Do you know anything else about possible side effects from my outer body ability?"

"Why? Are you feeling alright?" Octavio stood up and walked to Luke.

"I'm good. I was just wondering . . ."

"You miss it?"

"Uh, yeah. How'd you know?"

"I've been told by other angels who possess this power that it can happen. Especially when the power is new. It leaves you with a euphoric feeling, you can be lured into trying it again. Is that what you're experiencing?"

Octavio sat next to Luke.

"I feel out of place in my own skin. Like I'm being pulled. A part of me wants to be free to glide wherever I want to go. Be released from the confines of humanity. I guess I'm not really human either."

"The stronger you become the more you will be able to manage and eventually master your gifts. Since this feeling is strong, I wouldn't suggest any more out of body trips for a while. Only if it is absolutely necessary."

Luke nodded his head in agreement. Octavio got up and engaged in a whispered conversation with Rufus. He suspected Octavio hadn't told him everything he knew about this particular gift, but he didn't have the strength for confrontation.

Nestling closer to Mary, he squeezed her hand slightly and then kissed it. She gazed into his eyes, her wistful smile summing it all up.

"You agree with Octavio?" Luke's fingers tickled the back of Mary's hand.

"If it's too dangerous, then yes. But I also think you're the only one who make that decision."

"It's a lot."

"I know."

Abruptly Octavio stopped talking and put his hand over his mouth to signify silence. He walked to the right side of the tunnel and placed his hand on the wall.

"They're coming. Lilith and Samael will be here soon."

Luke pushed against the wall and rose to his feet. "I hear them too. Is that one of your super-powers?"

"I've picked up a few of them along the many years I've been around." Octavio raised a brow.

"Yeah, and just how long has it been, Octavio?"

"Perhaps that is a story for another day."

Octavio peered down the tunnel with a flashlight. He stood waiting until he heard Lilith and Samael coming toward him.

"They're almost here but I hear Lilith and she sounds—"

"Out of breath." Luke interjected.

Mary jumped to her feet. "I'm going down there. Luke, do you have enough strength to light the tunnel?

Luke jumped to his feet, standing next to Octavio and raised his hands toward the darkness. The passage lit up giving Mary a clear view. She took off running.

Luke waited, riddled with anxiety in his weakened state. He wanted to help but his body felt like it had been dragged behind a car for several blocks. When Mary called to them, he relaxed.

The huddled forms at the end of the tunnel drew closer, Lilith supporting Samael on one side and Mary the other. They brought him into their makeshift den and set him down.

Samael twisted, positioning himself against the wall.

"How is everyone? Luke, you look weak, son."

"I'll be okay. Just adjusting my body." Luke grinned.

"Be careful. That skill can be overpowering in the beginning."

"I know." He darted a look at Octavio. "I've been schooled."

"You hurting, Samael?" Luke was concerned.

"A little. But it'll pass soon. Lilith explained what happened. Damn Araqiel, he's like gum on a shoe." Samael winced.

Lilith sat down beside Luke and nudged his shoulder with hers.

"We're all together and fairly unscathed so that's a plus."

Luke smirked. "Way to see the upside."

"Hey kid, this could be worse."

"Yeah, I know. It's just that I'm starting to feel like this was a bad idea."

"What was?"

"Coming down here. They can still reach us. At least if we were above ground, we'd have more places to hide." Luke sighed.

Octavio interjected. "We will be safe for most of the trip from now on. The walls are sturdy, and the protection prayer is intact. It will get sketchy again when we near our destination.

But by then we will be in close proximity to Michael and his army."

"Well, that's good news." Luke grinned.

"Hopeful." Mary whispered.

Luke was the first to regain full strength. About thirty minutes later, Samael followed. To preserve Luke's abilities, they opted to use the flashlights to light their path.

The trip was long and the heat in the tunnels baked the moisture from their skin, leaving it dry and itchy.

Luke ferociously scratched his forearms. "This won't stop."

Mary took his arms and gently blew up and down. "Does that help?"

"Thanks, it does." He pressed his forehead to hers. "Darkness and light, brings dawn."

"Better together." She kissed his cheek.

"Okay Buffy and Angel, let's keep moving." Lilith waved her hand.

"Angel and who?" Luke raised a brow.

"It's a '90's tv show, but Lilith, Angel was a vampire and Luke couldn't be more different," retorted Mary.

"Oh jeez, this wasn't literal. They were a young couple in love."

"Actually, wasn't Angel really old?"

"That's it. I'm done. Samael, you wanna help me out?" Lilith rubbed her temple.

"I think you're on your own, I have no idea of what you're talking about."

"Never mind, let's just all walk."

Their conversations became sparse, which helped to preserve their energy for walking. The longer they pushed on the sooner they'd reach safe haven.

Luke was in awe of this part of the tunnel, every wall was covered from ceiling to floor with the prayer that kept them out of harm's way. Occasionally he would run his fingers along the etched words as he passed by. He tried to envision the men who'd constructed the tunnel, but he couldn't. It would've been a cool ability though.

His sense of being a part of something important was overwhelming. The scope of who he was, and who his family were, as well as the lives they lived gave him hope that they could win.

A renewed light seized his spirit and quickened his pace.

"Hey, slow down. You're gonna get tired too quickly," Mary huffed.

"Sorry. All of a sudden, I had this burst of excitement."

Samael joined in. "What were you thinking about?"

"What does that have to do with anything?"

"Your body is changing. As each day passes you get closer to Fulfillment. Everything is heightened. Your senses, your awareness. Everything around you will become clearer and more concise. So—what were you thinking about? Whatever it was it caused a reaction that exhilarated you and a power to push."

"I was just wondering about the Guardians who worked on the walls. What dedication and strength they must have had. You said the prayers were written in Aramaic, where did they come from?"

"Most of them are from the time that Jesus walked the earth. A compilation of Jewish text from their scrolls and recordings created into prayers. That's what the men did who etched the words into the stone. After it was complete, it was blessed by leaders of our order." Octavio gazed up toward the cavern ceiling. "Did you feel the power of those before you?"

"What are you talking about?" Luke asked.

"You've been touching the walls. You are a part of this—a crucial element to the plan. Just as the men who created these prayers were. You're connected to each other. The stronger you become, the stronger the connection. Now slow down. Mary's right, you'll tire too quickly if you keep that up."

They slept during the day and walked at night, marking each day as a victory that brought them closer to the end. Eating enough to keep up their strength but not consume the food supply too quickly was difficult. Luke rubbed his gut, the sour taste in the back of his throat was a reminder of the emptiness he couldn't fill. He envisioned a giant order of fries next to a thick burger and a glass of cola, sometimes it helped and other times, not so much.

They spent twenty-two days underground with no incidents. Luke was dusty, sweaty, and smelly. They used little pop-up wipes that each of them had stashed in their backpack, but it wasn't enough to combat the length of time that had passed without a shower.

Mary crinkled her nose. "We're all getting so ripe—the demons should be able to find us by smell."

"Speak for yourself, I smell like a man." He smirked.

"Sure, if the man rolled around in a pile of garbage and stepped in dog poop, then yeah, you do." Mary rolled her eyes.

On the evening of the twenty-sixth day, things started to change. The engravings on the walls were showing subtle signs of interruption. Luke pointed it out to Octavio who just nodded his head in agreement. Luke wasn't sure what he expected from him, but it seemed more important to him than to be dismissed with just a shake of the head. The further they walked the more apparent it was that they would soon be in trouble.

"I thought we'd be closer before this started."

"We should. There's about a day's journey where the walls are like this, but after that it will get better. Just stay aware—all of you."

Mary looked weary.

"How are you holding up?" Luke used a soft tone.

"Well let's see . . . I haven't showered in over three weeks. We're basically surviving on squirrel food and my father is a hitman for Satan. How am I holding up? Great. How about you?"

"Sarcasm?"

"Yeah, well that's all you're getting right now." She knitted her brows.

"Fair enough."

"How are *you* doing?" Mary squeezed Luke's hand.

"I think you pretty much said it for the both of us. I'm worried. These walls aren't looking so good."

"I know. It's creepy." Mary frowned.

Lilith shouted abruptly. "Hey, you two, keep up with us. I don't want to be too far apart. There's strength in numbers."

"Lilith something's been bugging me." Luke and Mary quickened their pace.

"What's that?"

"How exactly is Mary supposed to get to Lucifer?"

Lilith averted her eyes to Samael and then to Octavio.

"What? Am I missing something?" Luke reached for Lilith's arm.

"Lilith, please tell him or I will." Mary narrowed her eyes.

Lilith straightened her back and turned to face Luke. "Araqiel will be able to open a portal through the sparse placement of the surviving protection spells and then he will snatch Mary. They'll bring her to Lucifer."

Luke jumped back from Lilith like she was patient zero in the zombie apocalypse. His eyes grew wide as he clenched his fists at his side.

"What the fuck is wrong with you people? You didn't tell me, why?"

"Because of this," said Lilith. "We wanted to spare you."

"Spare me? Do you think I'm a child who can't handle anything? When?"

Mary stepped closer and looked longingly into his eyes. "It'll happen soon."

"You knew?" Luke's jaw tightened.

"Yes." She held his gaze.

"And what—you were just going to let yourself get snatched? Do you even have a plan for getting close to Lucifer, or are you just going to wing it?"

Mary looked to Lilith, but Luke placed his finger under her chin and turned her face toward him.

"Please. Look at me. What is the damn plan?"

Mary's tears trickled down her cheeks, and she wiped them with the sleeve of her shirt. Clearing her throat, she pulled her shoulders back.

"After I'm captured, I'll make my father think I'm accepting my dark side. When Lucifer arrives, I meet the asshole. After I gain his trust and when the time is right, I'll plunge the blade into his heart."

"I have a question?" Luke leaned forward and stood no more than three or four inches from her face. "How do you plan on gaining Lucifer's trust?"

Lilith interjected. "Luke. We don't have time for this now."

Without breaking her attention from Luke, Mary stopped Lilith. "He deserves to hear all of it. Luke, you knew this was happening. Even if you didn't know about me being taken from the tunnels. How did *you* think I was going to get close to Lucifer? Did you think he would just welcome me with open arms? I will do *whatever it takes* to get to him. This isn't a game. We don't get second chances. Don't you get it? *This* is my test. There is no other choice. I didn't want to deceive you, none of us did. But it was the best way."

He knew, deep down inside he felt it. He had chosen denial. "I didn't want to . . ."

Mary caressed his cheek. "I get it."

Luke looked away. The thought of losing her shattered him, but he knew the prophecy.

"Know this. When you do face him, we'll be fighting our way through his army to get to you. Promise me something, though."

"What is it?"

"Don't die." Luke looked away from her.

This time it was her turn. She clasped his chin and turned him to face her again. "You know I can't make that promise."

"Mary . . ." Her name was a loud boom that resonated through tunnel.

Startled, Luke's wings opened, and Samael's followed. Luke used them to envelope Mary as Samael shot through the tunnel in the direction of danger. Lilith, Octavio, and Rufus pulled their weapons free and were in a fighting stance. In moments Samael came back, nearly hitting the wall before stopping.

"They're here. Several of those ogres and I think Araqiel."

"My father? Down here?" Mary pulled away from Luke's protective cocoon. "It's my time." She turned to Luke.

"No. It's too soon. We have days before we reach Michael."

He tried to hold her, but she broke free. Before they had time for any more arguing, six ogres plunged down the tunnel and leapt into the air smashing into everyone except Mary. Fighting furiously, they each tried their best to stay up.

"My beautiful daughter."

Araqiel appeared, standing in the midst of the chaos.

"Father."

"It's time we end this. Come with me." He extended his hand.

"What about my mother and friends?"

"If you come with me quietly, I promise they will live—for now. Fight me and each defiance will add to their suffering."

"Mary, don't!" Luke lunged for her but was held back by the grip of one of the Ogres.

"Luke, it's okay."

"No!"

Araqiel shouted a retreat to his small band of beasts. Grabbing Mary, he lifted them both up and hovered for a moment sneering at Luke.

"You've lost her, boy. You'll lose this war, and I will sit at the right hand of my Dark Prince and laugh as they pull you apart piece by piece while your father watches."

"Be seeing you, Araqiel. Keep looking over your shoulder. I won't be far behind." Luke glared.

Spinning, Araqiel created a funnel of air and then swooshed out of the tunnel with Mary.

Luke was bleeding from a large gash on his cheek and the others nursed similar minor wounds. He gazed up. The flashlight gave enough light for him to catch a row of symbols patterned across the ceiling. With arms outstretched he illuminated the area. A new set of symbols—different than those on the walls—covered the ceiling.

"Lilith. Take a look at this."

Lilith leaned back. She traced the symbols in the air with her index finger. "Octavio, what are those?"

"I have no idea." He looked to Rufus who appeared to be just as confused as he was.

"Samael, do you recognize them?"

"That is the language of angels. But it is forbidden to use it outside of heaven."

Lilith abruptly rose. "Well then, what are they doing here?"

"Good question my love." Samael got up and stood beside Lilith. "These words are very powerful. They can be manipulated to carry out the will of whomever is using them. But they are only for the use of the archangels."

"Does Lucifer know them?"

"Yes. But he was forbidden from ever speaking or using them after he was cast out."

"Yeah, well he isn't the obeying kind of guy." Lilith paused. "What do they mean?"

"They open a portal."

"Like one that Araqiel might have used to get to us?"

"Exactly. The broken protection prayer on the walls made it easier for him."

"What other portals could it open?" Lilith's voice faltered. "Please don't tell me . . ."

"I know what you're thinking, and yes, it could open the gateway from hell if it were spoken correctly."

"We need to go. I think Araqiel and his demons will be preoccupied trying to open the gateway. We need to get to Michael—now!"

Octavio grabbed his pendant and mumbled words under his breath. As before, when he opened it for Lilith, a staircase appeared.

The trip up took longer than when they first entered the tunnels and they needed to stop a few times to catch their breath. Luke couldn't figure out how Lilith had made it up so quickly before. She had said it took about ten minutes and they seemed to be going for at least thirty already with no light in sight.

"I came out at a different place. It brought me back close to Samael's house. We weren't as far underground then."

"Okay. How the hell did you know what I was thinking?" Luke's eyes were wide.

"Thinking? You said it out loud."

"I did?"

Samael laughed. "You sure did."

Luke felt disorientated. He looked back at Lilith and the room began to spin. Losing his balance, he slumped over the railing. Samael slipped passed Lilith and reached out in time to catch him. Hoisting him over his shoulder he carried him the remainder of the climb. When they reached the opening, he laid Luke down on a bed of grass. He was awake but foggy.

Lilith knelt beside him and checked his arms and then rolled up his pants to look at his legs. Seeing nothing, she then lifted his shirt and with Samael's help, rolled him over to check his back. In the center, just below his shoulder blades was a huge burn mark etched into the flesh.

"Araqiel!" Lilith shouted out.

"This isn't good." Octavio took a small pouch out of his vest pocket. "I can treat it enough to keep it at bay, but we must get help."

"Samael, can't you do anything?" Lilith was shaky.

"I wish I could. This is the mark of an arch-demon. There is only one angel that can help him—Rita Peterson. Is she still in Boulder City?"

"Yes. Or at least she was the last time I spoke with Gabriel."

Octavio pulled out a small vial of cream. Putting some on his index finger, he smeared it all over the mark.

"St. Rita was in Boulder City?" Octavio grinned.

"You know her?" Lilith placed her backpack under Luke's head.

"Very well. She is a great healer. If anyone can fix Luke it is definitely her."

"Octavio, why do I get the feeling you are leaving something out?"

"Never you mind, Miss Lilith. We should get the boy to a more comfortable place."

"Right. I'm going to call Gabriel. Chances are he and Cassie will be coming. Samael can you rent a room somewhere nearby?"

"I'll need a phone."

"Look." Lilith pointed.

A small convenience store sat no more than 200 feet away, on the other side of a two-lane highway. Samael ran across the grassy patch and asphalt, returning in minutes. He Googled lodging in the immediate area. An EZ 8 Motel was a convenient half a mile away.

"Got us a room. Did you talk to Gabriel?"

"Yeah. They're on their way. And I was right, Cassie is coming. They should be here in a couple of hours."

"Hours? Why don't they just come now?" Samael sounded irritated.

"They don't want to tip off Araqiel's demons. With the ripples that angel flight causes, they'd be on them in a second." Lilith explained.

"You're right." Samael agreed. He picked up Luke with ease and bound for the motel.

NINE

Gabriel set his cell phone down and hugged his wife. "He's going to be okay. We'll get there and Rita will heal him." Gabriel said reassuringly.

Cassie nodded. "I'll see if Becca can stay with Karen."

"I'm going to talk to the Peterson's." Gabriel grabbed his keys off the coffee table.

"I'll meet you back here in twenty minutes." Cassie ran upstairs to pack a bag for Becca.

The Peterson's were friends and would do anything to help, but this was the worst timing. With all the kids training and going through procurement, they were needed in Boulder City. But Gabriel knew Rita was the only one who could help.

He sat in their kitchen and asked them to leave their own family to save one of his.

Rita Peterson gazed out to the backyard where her two youngest sons Marcus and Jonas were honing their combat skills.

"Gabriel, you know Luke is like one of our own. We'll be packed and ready to go in thirty minutes. Jason can keep an eye on the kids."

"I thought Jason was meeting up with Michael tomorrow?"

Gabriel inquired.

"The plan changed. Mary has been taken. Michael wants Jason to finish procurement so he can reach fulfillment. He'll leave in a week or two and he'll be a better asset then. I feel better knowing he'll be here while we're gone.

"I can heal Luke quickly, and we'll be right back. We'll meet you in front of your house."

Gabriel hurried home and informed Cassie that the Peterson's would be there shortly. Cassie let out a sigh of relief. In her heart, she knew they'd be there for her son, but she also knew the danger of leaving the children behind and essentially unguarded. She wouldn't have blamed them if they had refused to help.

The Peterson's were waiting out front when Gabriel and Cassie came out. The four piled into Gabriel's Jeep Wrangler.

"Where are we headed?" Rita clasped her seat belt. Peering through the rearview mirror, Gabriel replied. "San Jose."

The room was small, but clean. Samael set Luke down on one of the two queen-size beds. Octavio and Rufus opted for the floor. They rolled out their sleeping bags, lay down and closed their eyes. Lilith lay on her back on the other bed with the phone by her side while Samael took a seat by the window to keep watch.

No sooner had Lilith drifted off than the phone buzzed. Samael turned his attention to Lilith as she sat on the edge of the bed.

"Okay. Yes. It's the EZ 8 Motel on 1st street. Uh huh . . . sure. I understand. Five o'clock. He's unconscious right now. I think it's better that way. Octavio alleviated his pain. It only bought us a little time though."

Lilith hung up.

"What did he say?" Samael opened the drape a few more

inches.

"They're on the next flight. It'll take them about three hours. I just hope Luke can hold on that long." Lilith brushed the back of her hand across Luke's cheek.

"He's young and strong. He'll make it."

"I don't know. I only heard about this, and it was a long time ago. I've never seen the actual mark. A friend lost her sister to the arch-demon, Asmodeus."

"The same demon that cursed Cassandra?" Samael raised a brow.

"One and the same. He's a real evil bastard. Right up there with the entire unholy council."

"Nonetheless. Luke will be fine. I feel it. His heart is beating strong—he's fighting it. They will get here in time and Rita will heal him. Then we can all go to Michael and the others."

"I wonder how far we are from Portland?" Lilith Googled the route on the cell.

"I wish we there already." Samael leaned back on the chair.

"The route shows it should take us about ten hours to get there." She set her phone down on the nightstand.

"If we leave first thing in the morning, we'll be there by tomorrow night."

"That's if Luke is ready."

"Once Rita heals him, we can put him in the back of the car." Samael stood up and stretched his legs.

"And what car is that Samael?"

"The one I'm going to be taking from Gabriel when they get here." Samael grinned.

"You are purely devilish at times."

"Impossible, I'm an angel of light. No evil runs in these veins."

"You don't have veins."

"A small oversight."

"Okay enough of the angel humor. I'm getting some sleep

while I can. You sure you're okay with first watch?"

"I require much less shut eye than you, my little human."

"Whatever. Wake me in a few hours, please."

"Sleep well." Samael walked over and grabbed a corner of the bedspread and pulled it up over Lilith's legs. She was snoring lightly in five minutes.

The plane took off with a bumpy ascension. Gabriel nervously clutched both arm rests with white knuckles. Cassie chuckled.

"You fly to what heights with nothing but your wings to keep you in the air. And a little turbulence makes you crazy?"

"It's not the turbulence, per-say. It's the fact that I am not in control of this flight. If something were to go wrong, I could very well get myself and you out of this plane and safely to the ground. As could Rita and Peter. But what of all these other souls on board? Look around, there are children on this flight."

Cassie scanned the plane and looked at the faces of those who were, but a moment ago, just bodies on a plane. She felt a ping in her stomach and understood Gabriel's fear.

"I understand. I really do. But we can't control everything around us. You can't save everyone on this planet from harm. If it is the will of God, then it is what will be. You know this as well as I do. We have to hope that for today, on this flight, everyone is meant to arrive at our destination safely."

"I know, but humans are so fragile. Even you. I see the pain you can experience. It is far worse than anything me or any of my brothers or sisters will ever know."

"How about you focus on our son. I think that's something we can fix for today."

"You're right."

Gabriel lay his head back on the seat and gazed out the window. He longed to spread his wings and soar.

TEN

Luke eyed Mary in the distance. She was screaming, her body thrashing back and forth, slamming repeatedly into a concrete wall. He tried to run to her, but his legs wouldn't move. Narrowing his eyes, he frantically searched for what or who was doing this, but all he saw was her broken body. He tried to unfurl his wings—nothing. He tried to concentrate on her and leave his body, but he was powerless. He yelled to her, but she didn't respond. Furiously, he thrashed his arms, trying to break free of his unseen restraints. He grew more and more breathless. Gasping, he heard someone calling to him from a distance. Turning his head from side to side, it was barely recognizable. Was it his mom? Not seeing anyone, he collapsed on the ground while the last bit of air escaped his lungs. Then, with a jolt, his soul was ripped from his body. "Luke! Luke! Wake up. We're here. Come on, look at me." Cassie had tears rolling down her cheeks.

"Mmmom?" Luke's eyes fluttered.

"Let me get to him." Rita gently moved Cassie aside.

Someone rolled Luke on his stomach, he couldn't see them, but their presence felt familiar. He shivered from the placement of cool hands on the center of his back. In the distance, far from his reach, the whispering of the divinity prayer echoed in his head. He recognized the voice—Rita.

A heat grew in his belly vining its way through his torso and limbs. He tried to move but he couldn't. He labored to push words past his lips but all he could manage was a gurgle stuck in the back of his parched throat.

Rita's hands lifted and with them the heat that captured his body. His temperature quickly returned to a comfortable setting. He tried wiggling his fingers, one by one movement came back. He heard Samael's voice echo in the room.

"Gabriel, we'll need your car."

"I figured as much." Gabriel turned to Octavio and Rufus, his voice grating with anger. "Explain something to me. How is it the two of you allowed this to happen? From what I'm told, there have been many mishaps on this journey. I expected Araqiel to try his damnedest but Samael and Luke both came too close to death. What exactly is it you're guarding? Because it's not them." Gabriel stepped back. He was too heated and didn't trust himself.

Luke tried to turn on his side to face his dad, but his body was too heavy and his limbs too weak.

Lilith interrupted. "Listen, they fought just as hard as we did. They risked their asses for all of us. Look at them. Do they appear to be unscathed by the whole thing? They're just as bruised and banged up as we are."

Luke whispered, "It's not their fault." But no one heard him.

"They are supposed to be skilled. This is their purpose." Gabriel huffed.

"You're upset. I get that. But you can't blame them. Araqiel sent a form of human I'd never seen before. The Guardians did their job under unexpected circumstances. We all did. Demons are strong but these things are ten times the strength of anything we've ever encountered before." Lilith's tone was bitter.

This is all wrong, no one's to blame but Araqiel. I have to make my dad hear me. Luke winced; his throat roared back at him every time he tried to choke out the words.

Gabriel paused, looking at the cuts and dried blood that covered Octavio and Rufus's arms and face.

"I apologize. This was much easier when we didn't have our own children to worry about."

"Tell me about it. My daughter is on her way to Lucifer. My heart feels like it's breaking." Lilith put her hand on Gabriel's shoulder.

"We'll get her back. Mary is strong and very smart. She will get this done. When Mary plunges the blade into his flesh, she will send him to the underworld forever. The curse will never allow him to surface again," said Gabriel.

"I know. But she's only seventeen." Lilith turned to Samael and put her head on his shoulder. He wrapped his arms around her in an embrace and kissed the top of her head. She snuggled close.

Luke's legs shifted slightly as he tried to move them to the side of the bed, he outstretched an arm, but it fell, draping over the edge of the bed.

"Luke!" Cassie exclaimed.

"Mom . . . Dad." The pain was worth brief communication.

Luke grabbed his neck and pointed to a bottle of water on the nightstand.

Fumbling, Cassie opened the bottle and brought it to her son's lips. Slowly, Luke let the liquid coat the raw burning in his throat, bringing freedom to his voice.

"I saw Mary." His voice scratched out the words. "She was in trouble. Something was killing her. We have to get to her. She's in trouble."

"No. Quiet down. Mary's not dying. They took her as

planned. It was a bad dream, a side effect from being infected. That's all."

"My head feels like it's been slammed against the wall." Luke massaged his temples.

Rita came over and checked his eyes. "It will pass shortly. Just stay still; it was a very powerful curse. Its effects will take some time to leave your system."

Cassie glanced over to Rita. "Thank you, for saving our boy's life."

Rita smiled and nodded.

"We leave tonight, I got us a flight back in a few hours." Gabriel scrolled through his phone. "I wish we could stay son, but . . ."

"It's okay, we're gonna do this." Luke winced. "Mary's gonna get that unholy reject."

"You're not a boy anymore. Look who became a man while he was away." Cassie brushed away strands of hair from her son's face.

"Mom." Luke bellowed.

"Come on Cassie. He needs to rest. Who's hungry?" Gabriel asked.

The group shouted *me* in unison.

"Well, I think we need to order some pizzas."

Gabriel scrolled through some of the local pizza restaurants until he came to Lenny's.

Two large pepperoni, a large mushroom, hot wings and three liters of Coke were devoured within twenty minutes of being delivered.

"Best pizza on the west coast." Gabriel rubbed his belly.

Cassie rolled her eyes. "Are you sure you tasted it? For someone who doesn't need food, you sure make the best of earthly cuisine."

"What can I say—I adapt." Gabriel laughed.

Gabriel stepped outside under the canopy of midnight

blue; the crisp air chilled his bones, but he wanted to check the perimeter of the motel grounds. Peter and Lilith joined him while Samael stayed back to guard against unwanted visitors.

When they returned from their walk, Luke sat in a chair next to the small dinette table.

"We have to get to the airport, our flight leaves in three hours." Gabriel checked his phone then looked at Samael. "We'll take a cab, I'd feel better knowing you were here, at least until Luke is stronger."

Luke placed his hands on the table and used it as leverage to stand up.

Cassie embraced her son and held him tight. He knew his mom was worried but there wasn't anything he could do to change it. Becca needed her mother. She was immortal, like their mother, and needed her guidance.

"When will Becca be traveling to Michael?"

"She's almost ready. She can call on her visions at will and the headaches are mostly gone. Michael is counting on her sight to light the way for Mary. Hopefully, she will be able to give her the advantage she needs to strike at the right time."

"Tell her I love her." Luke pulled back from his mom, stepping away he felt the impact of such a subtle move. This was his journey now, his fate laid in his own hands. He couldn't rely on his mother's protection.

Luke opened his eyes when he heard Samael at the door.

"I'm going to do a quick perimeter check again, go back to sleep." Samael slipped out.

Laying in the darkness of the quiet room, Luke reflected on the events of the past ten months. His life before seemed to be no more than a dream. The things that were so important—

football, playing a great game for the college scouts—they were all trivial now.

His thoughts traveled to Mary and the day they met. He'd known the moment he saw her that she was different.

Rolling to his side he stared at the wall. It was blank, like their future. He told his mom everything would soon be normal, but the truth was he had no idea how this was going to turn out. Like the empty wall, the possibilities were vast and most of them sent a shudder up his spine. And *normal,* that would have an entirely new meaning when all of this was done. He was fooling himself if he thought they'd just go back to life on Ramona Lane as if nothing had happened. He was changed. They all were. Closing his eyes, he let his dreams take him to a secure place . . . in Mary's arms.

There were no nightmares and Luke slept hard until the headlights of a car beamed through a gap in the drapes. The lights danced along the Formica top of the nightstand beside the bed, spotlighting a bright white across his face. He looked over at the window. It was still dark outside. Lilith stood beside the other queen-sized bed packing their belongings.

"You weren't kidding when you said we were leaving early." Luke yawned.

"Yup. We'll grab something to eat once we're on the road. Don't leave anything behind, okay?"

"I will. I mean, I won't leave anything." Luke was still groggy.

"I know what you meant."

After she was done getting her backpack together, Lilith checked every corner of the room to make sure no evidence remained. Even the smallest detail would be enough for demonic soldiers to get a picture of where they might be headed. Dealing with supernatural hunters was a whole different game than those of humankind. She had once seen a tracker find someone merely from a crumpled-up fast food receipt. The poor soul had left enough of an imprint that the maniacal hunter could get a vision of their thoughts. He had caught up and shredded him in less than a day. Hell didn't care if they were captured dead or alive. They did enjoy alive though, so they could torture their captives before ending them. But the real torture started in death—when Lucifer claimed his reward.

"Octavio, can you wash the room of our essence?" Lilith sighed.

"As soon as you all leave."

Lilith motioned for all of them to shuffle out of the room. When it was empty, Octavio took a vial out of his pocket and, standing just outside of the doorway, he splashed it into the room and around the framework. He repeated the words, "Please cleanse all that is contained within these walls that we have touched or used. Please assign Your holy angels to protect us during our journey."

Luke turned to Lilith. "Exactly how many of those vials does he carry?"

"Many." She gave him a disapproving glare.

"That's it? He's done?" Luke expected more.

"That'll do it. A simple task can save your life, but many souls forget to cleanse away the evidence they were there. That's how they get caught. Which is why I told you to make sure you don't leave anything behind."

"I didn't."

"I know. I checked." Lilith smirked.

Luke ignored the salty comment.

Gabriel had rented an SUV with all the bells and whistles. Thinking about Samael's car collection, Luke wondered if it was an angel thing. He laughed to himself. They could fly but loved their cars.

Lilith drove with Samael next to her. Rufus and Octavio took the seats behind them, and Luke sprawled out on the two in the very back. He was still sluggish from remnants of the curse that Araqiel had placed on him.

Daydreaming about the time he took a shot in the open field and scored a winning touchdown; Luke was startled back to reality by a loud boom. His body flung into the door and his head knocked against the window.

"Luke. Put on your damn seatbelt." Samael demanded.

Fumbling for each piece, he quickly got himself harnessed in. He caught a glimpse of Lilith in the rear-view mirror. Her wide eyes said it all.

A loud thud to the rear of the vehicle stole Luke's attention, he spun his head around in time to see the demon Astaroth clinging to the back of the SUV. Clenching the trunk, the demon slithered his body across the glass of the rear window and onto the roof. Abaddon was in flight right behind him.

"Lilith!" Luke yelled out.

"I know! I know!"

"I need to go out there. They're not going to stop." Samael released his seat belt.

"They'll kill you." Lilith was frantic.

"I can get rid of them. I've done it before."

"Yes, but we had Mary's help." Luke chimed in.

Samael flung open his door. "I'm going."

Luke saw the enormous spread of feathery wings as Samael soared up into the clouds. He watched as the angel spiraled down like a tornado and slammed into Abaddon, knocking him from flight onto the highway. The demon rolled into an oncoming car and rested motionless on the side of the road.

While Astaroth pounded the roof, Samael circled above gaining speed. Coming down headfirst, he grabbed the demon with both hands and thrust him into the steel blue. Astaroth gained his control and swooped up into the clouds and out of sight. Luke searched out of the back window for signs of

Abaddon. The other half of the demonic duo had regained his senses and was once again headed straight for them.

"I have to go help him." Luke unbuckled his seatbelt.

"Are you crazy? You're not going out there. Luke, you're not ready for this."

"Come on, Lilith. I've already faced both of them."

"And as you pointed out, we had Mary's help. This is full aerial combat—different than anything you've done."

"I have to help."

Before Lilith could say another word, Luke had the door open and was gone.

He unfurled his wings; it felt good. He ascended, gaining momentum before redirecting his flight toward Abaddon. Ready for the fight, Abaddon met Luke halfway and slammed him off balance, sending him twirling toward the open sky. This time however, Luke was quick to recover and barreled into the demon's side. Pushing with the full weight of his wings, he slammed Abaddon into the trunk of a tall palm tree and then pulled back with a right hook to the surprised demon's face. He pinned him with his left hand and repeatedly jabbed him in the gut with the right. The light from his brothers and sisters nourished his soul, making him stronger and more precise. Each punch landed harder than the last.

The demon's body shriveled up and slumped over. Luke released him and he plummeted to the ground. This time he wasn't taking any chances. He grabbed a thick branch from a neighboring Oak tree and ripped it from the trunk. Shooting toward the heavens, he circled, gaining speed with every lap until he shot like an arrow searching for its mark. Holding up the limb of the tree Luke slammed it straight into Abaddon's skull. Tissue and bone fragments splintered into the air, landing in chunks around the mangled body.

Not wasting any time, Luke scouted the skies for Samael and Astaroth. Catching a glimpse of movement behind parting clouds, he headed up. Glancing back at the SUV, Lilith had pulled over to the side of the road. Standing beside the vehicle, she waved for him to come back, but he turned and ignored her. He felt stronger than he ever had, and he wanted to share that with Astaroth. In fact, he needed to. It was roiling his insides and he needed a release. What better way than to pulverize another demon's face. His speed intensified when he saw Samael and Astaroth in a mid-air battle the demon seemed to be winning. Luke shot straight through the middle of them creating an explosion that catapulted both in opposite directions.

Immediately, he set a course for Astaroth. The demon spun out of control and onto nearby power lines. Luke wasn't sure where Samael was, but he didn't have time to check. He wanted to reach the abomination from Hell before he freed himself from the entanglement. With the precision of a finely tuned instrument, Luke sliced more of the wires from the power line and circled the demon wrapping him tighter and more securely. When he was sure Astaroth couldn't break free, he ripped the ends of the lines from the pole sending the demon hurtling to the ground, embedding him into the asphalt.

Luke landed in a battle stance next to the moaning disciple of hell. The ground around him crumbled and large pieces of asphalt had flipped up onto his chest. Luke flicked them off with ease. Astaroth tried to pull his fractured body from the rubble, but his legs were broken.

"You think this is it, boy? Killing me won't change a thing. My Prince will be here soon, and all this will be gone. I will be rewarded for my service when I return home. You are nothing. A misguided angel who thinks his efforts are going to save the world."

"I may be nothing, but I am the one who is going to kill you."

Luke picked up one of the larger pieces of asphalt and slammed it down into Astaroth's neck, breaking it. Not satisfied, he jammed it in repeatedly until his head lay severed from his body.

He walked over to a grassy patch and sat down.

Samael ambled over and sat next to him.

"I saw what you did—all of it. You were fierce. Are you okay?"

"Never better. I had so much strength running through me. It was like I harnessed all the power in heaven."

"In a way, you did." Samael lay back and gazed up.

"What do you mean?"

"I saw the light descend from above and encircle you. You were touched by our brothers and sisters. You were fighting with the strength of a hundred angels."

"That explains the feeling. I knew there wasn't anything I couldn't conquer in those few minutes."

"Few minutes? Luke, they've graced you. It's yours for eternity. I think we can consider this your Fulfillment."

"What?" Luke stood up.

Samael lifted his head and used his hand to block the suns' rays.

"You are complete."

Lilith came backing up with the SUV and Octavio and Rufus jumped out.

"Are you alright?" Rufus checked Luke's face.

"I'm fine. Better than fine—I'm great."

"He's scratched up. I'll get a first aid kit."

Rufus disappeared into the back of the car and emerged with a small white box. He asked Luke to sit down and knelt next to him with the open box on the grass. It was packed with bandages, antibiotic ointment, alcohol wipes and other wound care items. He ripped open one of the alcohol pads and cleaned the deep scratches on Luke's face, he pulled back.

"You just fought and killed two of the most notorious

demons from Hell and a little alcohol makes you wince?" Rufus let out a deep, jolly laugh.

Lilith got out of the car and grabbed some of the wipes from the kit. Sitting next to Samael she cleaned his face and neck.

"We will both heal shortly. Why are you cleaning our wounds?" Samael scoffed.

"Because we're human." Lilith smirked. "When Rufus is done with Luke, I suggest we get our asses back on the road. We still have a whole day drive in front of us."

Luke sat behind Lilith and Samael this time, listening as Samael told Lilith about Fulfillment. That was good with him. He didn't feel like talking about it. He wasn't quite sure what it meant for him and his future, but he knew he would find out soon enough. They would reach Michael by late evening and his part in this war would become clear. He knew it.

Once or twice he caught Lilith stealing a glance at him through the mirror. He looked away. Somethings were just better left in the shadows.

"Luke. Luke. Hey, where the hell are you?" Lilith shouted from the driver's seat.

"Huh? Oh, miles away. Why what's up?" Luke opened a bag of snacks and grabbed some peanut butter filled pretzels.

"We'll be there soon. How are you feeling?"

"I'm okay. Hey Rufus, could you please grab me a soda?"

Rufus reached around and opened the lid of the small cooler. He grabbed a can of cola and handed it to Luke.

"How much longer?"

"Uh. About ten seconds. We're here."

Lilith pulled off the main street to a dirt road. Luke's eyes traced the outline of a two-story house with a large white porch, trimmed in twinkle lights. The SUV pulled up to the front and

Lilith turned off the engine. Pressing into the headrest on the seat, she let out a long sigh.

Anxious to get out and stretch his legs, Luke nearly tripped on the way out.

"Careful. I don't need one of my warriors defeated by his own clumsiness."

Luke turned; the silhouette of a tall, statuesque man walked toward him. As he grew closer, he could tell by his wavy dark hair, it was Michael.

"Uh, just tired of sitting." Luke fidgeted nervously.

"I'll bet you are. You all must be starving and need a good stretch. Let's walk around to the back of the house. The kitchen is there, and we have dinner waiting. Leave your things. Josiah will take them in."

A young boy maybe eleven or twelve stood behind Michael. He flashed a toothy grin then started emptying their vehicle.

Michael took them on a short walk of the property. It felt good to be out of the car and get the circulation flowing in his legs. The crisp air carried the perfume of thyme and rosemary, it reminded Luke of his mother's garden back home. Brushing his fingers across the branches of the bristly herbs, he reveled in the simplicity. Rounding the garden to the back of the house, another large porch sat under the soft illumination of Edison bulbs, inviting them in. The kitchen glowed with bright lights, and inside two short, plump women, bustled about. Snow white hair framed the folds of wrinkles in their aging their faces —twins.

"Everyone, I'd like you to meet the two ladies who keep us all from starving. This is Daisy and Rose. Ladies, meet everyone."

Rose wiped her hands on the yellow half apron she had tied around her waist.

"Sit. Sit. We have some nice beef stew and cornbread. And Miss Lilith, Michael told us about your detriment for meat. My sister Daisy has prepared a lovely vegetable medley in sweet onion gravy over brown rice."

"Thank you. You didn't have to go through so much trouble. Really, I could have thrown together something myself. But I must admit, it sounds delicious. We haven't had a home cooked meal in several weeks. This is wonderful."

Michael left them to dine and unwind. Luke relaxed for the first time in over a month. He felt like he had a little bit of home with him. The sisters reminded him of Adrian and Lucy Michaels. Both angels, both seniors. They were the pseudo grandparents to every kid on Ramona Lane. He missed them.

"Lilith, do you think we'll be here long?"

"Not sure. I don't know what Michael has laid out for all of us beyond the plan involving Mary. I do know the time is coming that we will face off in battle. It's inevitable. Even if— when—Mary sends Lucifer back to Hell his followers won't just lay down and die. We will have a war. I'm just not sure where." Lilith frowned.

Luke pushed the plate away from him and folded his arms on the table. "What if Becca doesn't get her full power in time? Is there a backup plan to save Mary without Becca's sight? I mean we can't just leave her with them."

"If Becca can't see her, I'll go and get her myself."

"You won't be alone."

"Agreed."

Luke pulled the plate closer and started eating. He didn't realize how hungry he'd gotten. Talking with Lilith, knowing they'd go for Mary eased his mind enough to let the hunger pang its way to his brain. He finished eating everything on his plate.

"It's so nice to have a boy with an appetite here.

"Isn't it Daisy?" Rose smiled at Luke.

"Oh, it's wonderful. Michael eats nothing. The others barely get by with a bite here and there. Luke, you make us proud." Daisy winked.

"Well, I'm glad you two ladies feel that way because I'll eat whatever you cook. If it's like this, I won't be able to get enough." He wiped his mouth with a napkin.

Lilith rolled her eyes and chuckled.

When they were finished Samael, Octavio, and Rufus joined Michael in the living room. Lilith soon followed. Luke waited, reveling in his last few moments of normalcy. Unfortunately, it wouldn't last. Michael called his name, summoning him to the gathering.

Luke traipsed into a crowded room. He stopped abruptly and leaned back; he hadn't seen anyone other than a handful of people when they first arrived. They must have come in through the front entrance when they were eating. Most of them were adults, men, and women his parents age or older. But a few were young like him. Luke felt a little out of place.

Michael had the young boy, Josiah, on his left side and he motioned for Luke to join them. Hesitantly he followed his request and took a stance to Michael's right.

"Good. Now we are all here."

"All of us? What about Becca and Jason . . ."

"Don't interrupt Michael when he addresses us." Octavio spoke in a sharp tone.

"That's all right. He's curious and has every right to be." Michael turned and faced Luke. "The plans have changed to accommodate events that have transpired in the last three days."

"What events?"

"Lucifer has risen and is back in Boulder City."

"We traveled all the way out here and now we're going back to Boulder City?"

"When we first found out about Lucifer's plan to rise, the primary cracks in the portal to Hell were about one hundred miles north of here. We estimated that with the number of demons escaping, Lucifer would be here shortly. The opposition started in Boulder City because Araqiel found out that was where the greatest number of angels were hiding. Your father picked that place because he thought it would be a good town for the families to blend in.

"We thought Araqiel and the others would look to the major cities because that is where we had resided through the centuries. We didn't plan on Mary."

"What about Mary?" Luke's voice dropped.

"Mary's lack of control over her dark and light side caused many issues for Araqiel. In order to avoid unwanted attention, he moved them many times. In fact, it was dumb luck that he settled in Boulder City. He had no idea any of you were there until he saw your face. You look amazingly like your father. Once he realized who you were, he put the plan in motion to seek out and destroy all of you. This would have been a big deal for him. To present the heads of all those angels to Lucifer upon his arrival would have secured his station in the army.

"I know my fallen brother. Trust does not come easily for him. Araqiel has failed. It won't be easy for him to reclaim a royal position in the devil's kingdom. He must be insane with intent. He will not stop until he can deliver all of us to his Prince."

"But what does all of this have to do with changing the plan?" Luke grew frustrated.

"Lucifer has been told of the congregation of angels in Boulder City and Araqiel's disappointing performance. They have managed to rip a large portal open somewhere out in the desert about seventy-five miles east of Boulder City. The walls of security are beginning to fall all over the world. He will rise there. We know it. My brother, who was once one of the most beautiful angels of us all has only one thing on his mind. He wants to destroy earth as it is and make it home for himself and all his depraved followers.

"With us out of the way it will be easier. But it runs deeper than that. He wants revenge for what he deems a betrayal by his brothers and sisters."

Luke huffed and then sat down on the floor. Crossing his legs, he put his head in his hands. Michael no longer made him nervous. These people no longer made him uncomfortable. He was exasperated.

"So, this was all for nothing. This trip—Mary. It was all pointless."

"No, Luke. The plan remains in place. Only the geography of the battlefield has changed. Mary will gain Araqiel's trust and then, ultimately, Lucifer's. She will do the job she has been born to do. Angels and demons are at war already all over this planet. But we will take the final stand in Nevada. And we must win. There is no alternative."

Quietly, Luke rose and walked outside. He needed to be alone and think it all through. The whole plan felt like one wrong turn after another. His head hurt and he laid down on an old wooden bench near the porch. He closed his eyes. If they were going back, at least he would be with his entire family and friends when the time came to wrestle the devil.

ELEVEN

They decided that drawing attention was less of a concern than getting to Boulder City quickly, so those with wings would fly. After assuring a plan was in place to protect the children of Ramona Lane, Lilith accompanied the humans as they drove in caravan formation.

Josiah was the youngest of the male angels and he shadowed Luke like a new puppy. Luke smiled to himself, the boy had a gleam in his eye, the luxury of innocence. Luke had been so wrapped up in everything that had happened to Mary, his parents, his friends, he'd almost forgotten how to be a kid. But the truth was he wasn't a kid anymore and, soon, Josiah would feel the same pain. But Luke had the power to prolong the boy's childhood as long as he could. Pulling him aside, they sat down away from the group so Luke could talk to him.

"How you doin?"

The boy eagerly hung on every word. "I'm great. I'm gonna fly with you."

"That's what I wanted to talk to you about. I need your help."

"You do?" Josiah's eyes grew wide.

"This is a big job and I'm not sure if you're willing to do it but, if you are, you'd really be helping me out."

"Okay!"

"I need you to fly with Tiberius."

Tiberius had come with a recommendation from Michael as being one of the more skilled of the group. Luke spoke to the teen earlier that evening and he'd agreed to watch out for the young angel.

"But I thought I was gonna be by your side?" The boy frowned.

"I know. I thought so too, and I'm kind of disappointed. But Tiberius needs someone with navigational skills, and I've been watching you . . . you got game. So, can you do this for me?"

"Okay Luke, if you need me."

"Oh great, that's a load off. Thanks."

The angels lined up wingspan distance from one another in a V formation. Tiberius gave Luke a nod when Josiah stood by his side. The beauty of fluent wings took to the heavens, stirring a gust of cool wind.

Deep navy sparkled in the distance under the illumination of copper orange, as they used the camouflage of evening clouds to conceal their journey. The bright cast of the full moon served as a headlight leading the way for the path home. Luke soaked it all in. The peace and quiet of this flight would soon be replaced with the sounds of war. Lucifer scared the hell out of him. But not as much as the thought he might never see Mary again. He'd stand up to the devil and fight with his last breath if it meant she would live through this. She hadn't ever known the love of family and friends. All Mary had was the maniacal Araqiel. She'd been robbed of the normal life she could have had with Lilith; her childhood was drenched in loneliness.

All he wanted for her was freedom to lead a normal life without being hunted like an animal to be used by both sides.

They were home by the time the sun shed its golden rays across the landscape of Boulder City as they danced across the mirror of Lake Mead. Flutters overtook Luke's belly the closer they got to Ramona Lane. He was anxious to see his friends again.

Gabriel greeted them in the driveway, embracing his son in a tight hug. They followed him to the backyard so they could talk.

"We found a few more of Lucifer's lackey's and Peter and I took care of them." Gabriel's smile was as cold and bitter like frost on a windowpane.

"I think we should forget about them for now and concentrate on Mary. We can dispose of the rest of them after we defeat Lucifer." Luke stood tall.

"I agree," said Michael. "Our energy is best used elsewhere."

Gabriel nodded his head.

"What about Becca? Any closer to connecting with Mary?"

"She has had a breakthrough and they've begun their own form of communication."

"Good, that makes me feel better." Luke huffed a breath. "I'm gonna go in and see her. Josiah, wanna come with me?"

"Sure." Josiah grinned.

"How you feeling? Tired?" Luke bumped the boy's shoulder.

"Kind of. But I'm okay."

"Maybe a short nap?" asked Luke

"I don't know."

Luke chuckled to himself. He knew the boy was exhausted, but he was not about to admit it.

After introductions and several hugs from Becca, Luke brought Josiah upstairs to lay down on Becca's bed for a while. He was practically asleep before his head hit the pillow. Luke quietly shut the door before going down to the kitchen to grab something to eat. Becca was waiting with a plate full of bacon, toast, and a glass of orange juice.

"Mom said you almost died." Becca's voice was shaky.

"I'm fine. Really."

Luke grinned at his little sister, but she wasn't so little anymore. Something had definitely changed about her.

"Don't do that." Becca was annoyed.

"What did I do?"

"Make it sound like it wasn't serious. You don't have to shield me. I know exactly what's going on. My visions make sure of that." Becca frowned.

"How does it work? Do you see it like a dream?"

"It's more like a movie and when I share it with Mary, I can send pictures that relate to the words I'm trying to say. We figured out a system pretty quick which was good because in the beginning it was confusing for her."

"Is it hard? I mean, knowing things?"

"It was at first. But now it's just sad. I know this is going to help us, but I wish I didn't see things so vividly."

"That's rough. But you're right, it will help us. You got this."

"Yeah. I know." Behind Becca's smile was great trepidation. "When you're done eating, dad left strict instructions for you to chill. We're all meeting this afternoon after Lilith arrives."

"Okay."

Luke gobbled up the remaining bacon and downed his juice before heading up to his room. He wanted time to think, Mary needed everything to go perfectly, and he wasn't about to disappoint her.

The sweat trickled from Mary's upper lip and she wiped the sting from her mouth. She knew the plan and hated it, but there was no other alternative.

"I said look at me." Araqiel's voice was as deadly as a well sharpened blade.

"What?" Mary said in a commanding tone.

"I told you to look at me when I speak to you."

She didn't give him the satisfaction. This was all part of the plan. She couldn't come around too quickly. Araqiel would know she was full of it if she did. No. It had to appear to be a process, her soul giving into the darkness within her. That would be the only way she could get close enough to Lucifer to do the deed.

"Why don't you go look at yourself? That's the only thing you truly love." She turned further from him.

"You are my daughter. Of course I care about how you feel. But I cannot have you disrespect me. Especially in front of our Prince."

"*Our* Prince? You're so misguided if you think I will do anything to give that thing any kind of loyalty."

"Enough!" Araqiel's voice was deepened with disgust.

Mary looked toward him and was startled to see the malformed body and wound ridden face that was once her father. She had witnessed his change once before, but it didn't make it any less terrifying. She found herself being pulled toward him with no means to fight back. His ability to control things around him with his mind was powerful. Her eyes grew wider with every inch her feet dragged across the floor. Once in his clutches, he grabbed her arm with a vice-like grip and raised her off the ground. She turned from his repulsive face, closing her eyes.

"You will listen to what I say, and you will be gracious about it. I cannot kill you, but— torture is an entirely different pleasure I can exercise."

Mary knew enough not to push him. In her heart, she also knew he meant what he said. How could she have lived with this monster all those years and not realized there was more to Araqiel than the obvious? Excuses—she always made them when it came to his behavior. To think, she actually felt sorry for him when she was growing up. *Poor Dad. He lost mom and had to raise her by himself. He was doing the best he could.* That's the lie she told herself over and over again.

"What's the matter? Nothing to say?" Araqiel snickered.

Mary turned and glared into Araqiel's eyes, but she did not respond.

"No need for you to speak. I know you are as anxious to see our Prince as I am. Or at least you will be. He will ascend in three days. Until then you have time to reflect on your choices. They are quite simple. You either give in and show him your undying love and worship or you die a torturous death. But not before you witness your beloved Luke being torn apart piece by piece. A delightful treat I will relish." Araqiel released Mary and she fell to the ground, bruising her arm. She rubbed it gently trying to get the blood flowing to relieve some of the pain. *Well, I got the part of detesting him played to perfection. Turning it around to make them believe I revere him is going to be harder.*

"Luke. Wake up."

Luke rubbed away the sleep from his eyes. His mom was sitting on the bed beside him.

"Time to join the rest of us in the backyard. Michael is waiting."

"Yeah. I'll be there in a minute. Just let me throw some water on my face." Luke fumbled with the covers.

She kissed the top of his head before leaving the room. He rolled out of bed and went to the restroom before ambling down the stairs and out to what appeared to be a hundred people gathered in his yard.

He took a place beside his friend Jason.

"Nice to see you again, brother," Jason said in a whisper.

"You too." Luke held up a fist to bump." You ready?"

"Yeah, I just want the devil to pay for everything's that's happened."

"Well, I'm guessing you're gonna get your wish."

"Yeah, Lucifer's somewhere in Nevada. We don't have any fix on his exact location yet, but we will. Becca's using Mary as a camera."

"Yeah, she explained it to me last night."

"I'm not sure how it works, but it's cool, right? It's just a matter of time before we figure out where the reject from Hades is hiding."

Michael stood front and center. In a military stance with his hands clasped behind his back, his stature emanating a proud royal.

"My family, I know what we are about to embark on will be war. We know Lucifer is already walking the earth, and in hiding in the desert. Mary doesn't know his location but does know he's expected in Boulder City in three days. Unfortunately, this means we wait. When the time is right, we will take up arms and fight. According to the visions, Mary will be our true savior. She has the most difficult job of us all. That is why I am appealing to all the angels in heaven and here today to give her wings. This might be the one procurement that could help keep her safe and ensure she can fulfill her destiny."

The angels nodded and Michael peered up into the sky.

"You hear me, brothers and sisters? Give the girl the tools she needs. She is fighting for us, for you, and all of humanity. Let her have the means to do so."

Michael raised up his arms to the heavens and then lowered his head. Luke scanned the yard. Everyone seemed to be waiting for some divine intervention, but nothing happened. Michael continued to look toward the heavens for a few lingering moments and then relaxed.

"It is done. I have made my request and now we will wait and hope for Mary's sake. In the meantime, training commences again and again until the third day. Rest, but only enough to keep up your strength. Many of you have never seen battle and certainly not one like this. Keep strong bodies and clear minds my brothers and sisters. Now go and prepare."

It didn't make sense. Why does Michael need to make a request for Mary's wings from the other angels? Was there some kind of angel council? Wasn't he their leader? The words in his head sounded ridiculous. Not wanting to wait or guess for an answer, he decided to go right to the source—Michael.

Luke scoured the grounds but couldn't find him, so he went inside and searched the house. Noticing the front door ajar, he peered outside. Michael, Uriel, and his father, were on the lawn in what appeared to be a heated discussion. His father seemed to be arguing while Michael adamantly shook his head in disagreement. He had his hand on the screen getting ready to crash their discussion when Michael roared a resounding, *No!* He shot straight for the clouds and out of site. Gabriel crouched to the ground and Uriel followed patting him on the back. Whatever it was they were arguing over had his dad clearly distraught.

Luke decided to confront Michael head on. He was growing anxious with the arch angel's surreptitious approach and as soon as he came back, they were gonna have a talk. While he was waiting, he tried out some new moves he watched Jason practicing earlier.

Finding a patch of the backyard that didn't have a warrior angel on it proved difficult, so he opted for the side of the house. No one was there and he had plenty of room to try out some aerial moves, his movement was choppy and clumsy.

"Well, that's a funny site. Luke Jacobs doing something badly."

Luke quickly spun around mid-air and then fell to the ground.

"Whoa. That had to hurt." Jason laughed heartily.

"Hey, pretty bad, right?"

"Don't get discouraged. I've been practicing these moves for six months now. You'll get it. Want some help?"

"I think I've got it." Luke's eyes gazed at the ground.

"There isn't time for this kind of crap. I know you're used to being on top of everything, but this is different. It's life or death and I prefer you stay on the living side of things. I'm sure Mary would agree. Let me help you."

Luke nodded. It was hard for him to relinquish control over something he thought should come easily to him. He had always been a star athlete just like his dad. Accepting help was a whole new experience.

"Show me what you got." Luke flashed an approving smile.

Jason shot up with the speed of a runaway train, racing toward the heavens he abruptly stopped, flipping head over heels until his body spun like the spin cycle on a washing machine. He slowed the pace and came to a halt. Outstretching his arms, he released his hold and plummeted toward the ground until he was only inches from slamming into the earth, hovering, he turned and grinned. "Good control, right?"

"Jeez, that was fast. But then again, you've always been like a damn cheetah on the field."

The two boys twirled and flipped repeatedly; it didn't take long for Luke to gain control of the manuevers that Jason had perfected. Yes, he fought Abaddon in a mid-air confrontation, but that was one on one. The battle he'll face now will be an army of demons, and he needed to be as skilled as his best friend in only a few days.

Luke swiped his forehead. "Hey, how about a water break?"

"Going soft on me?" Jason jabbed Luke's side.

"Give me a break. I'm jamming ten months into three days."

"Yeah, it's rough. I get it. Let's meet back here in ten, okay?"

"And I'll be ready to kick your ass."

"You can try." Jason hiked his brows.

Luke chuckled and ambled toward the house.

Michael was in the kitchen with a map of Boulder City spread out across the table. His blood grew hot when he remembered the frustration on his dad's face earlier.

"Michael, I need to talk to you." Luke wasn't asking permission.

"Yes, Luke. Come in and sit." Michael motioned toward the table and chairs.

Luke got closer but didn't sit. He wasn't giving in to any direction today.

"I want to know what you said to my father. He was clearly very upset. I also want to know if you are our leader like everyone keeps saying, why can't you just grant Mary her wings? Why do you have to ask other angels who, might I mention, aren't even down here helping us? This circle of secrets needs to end. We deserve to know what's going on. *Everything* that is going on."

Luke's voice cracked. His emotions were running wild, and he could no longer hold back his anger.

Michael stepped closer until he was towering over him. Luke squared his shoulders and swiped the palm of his hands down his pant legs. He knew the power Michael had, he listened to all the stories growing up. But if he showed fear, it would get him nowhere.

"I can understand your frustration. It may seem we're keeping secrets, but actually we are discussing strategy. We didn't want to share this with you and the others until we had our missions complete."

"Bullshit. You're the only one keeping secrets. And my father didn't look like he was discussing any strategy."

Another voice joined in. "But we were."

Luke turned and saw Gabriel standing in the doorway.

"Dad, you don't have to make excuses for him."

"I'm not. Michael is telling you the truth." Gabriel sat down.

"Gabriel there is no need to—."

"Yes brother, I do. Luke deserves the truth. The whole truth. Come here and sit with me."

Hesitantly he took a seat next to his father. Michael moved back toward the doorway and crossed his arms. His brow knitted in disapproval.

"The reason Michael and I were arguing was because we had a difference of opinion when it came to your role in this war."

"Me?" Luke's interest was piqued.

"Yes. An informant on the outskirts of town reported a bright glow coming from a cave about twenty miles from here. They believe it might be where part of Lucifer's army is waiting for his command. If we can make a dent in the fleet before the third day, it could give us a meaningful advantage."

"And how does this affect me?"

"I want you to lead the group that goes into the desert. Do some reconnaissance and see if our sources are correct. If they are, then you would engage and exterminate. Michael disagrees. He feels you are not ready yet and wants to send an older angel."

Luke's body thrummed with fortitude. He had mistaken what he saw in the yard, Michael was being protective of him.

"I appreciate what you were doing Michael, but my dad is right. I *am* ready. Besides, what difference is three days going to make in training? If I don't know it now, then I'm screwed."

"Language."

"Sorry, but it's true. Who is going with me?" Luke got up.

"I've assembled a group of twenty. They'll be ready to go when you are. Michael, I know you disapprove but I wouldn't be doing this if I weren't completely sure in my heart he was up to it."

"And Cassie? Have you told her?"

"She wasn't happy, but she has faith in my judgment. Something you once had."

Michael walked over and placed his hand on Gabriel's shoulder.

"I still do." Michael patted Gabriel's back.

"I should go get ready then. I'll be out front in about thirty minutes. I need to see Mom and Becca before I leave."

Luke took the stairs two at a time, the opportunity to kill demons exhilarated him—a side of his personality that scared and intrigued him. Changing into dark grey cargo pants, a long sleeve black t-shirt and black lace up boots, he checked his reflection in the mirror. A little cliché but it worked.

His mom was sitting on the bed in her room waiting for him.

"I'll be back."

"You better." She wiped her eyes.

He bent down and gave her a hug. "Love you, Mom."

Luke closed the door and went to Becca's room. It was empty. He searched the house before looking in the backyard. She was sitting by herself on one of the small settees.

"Hey kid, I'm leaving."

"I know."

"Gonna hug me goodbye?"

"Nope." Becca looked away.

"Why not?"

"Because if I hug you, we said goodbye."

"I see. All right then, I'll meet you in the kitchen for some ice cream tomorrow night."

Becca looked up. Her eyes were red and puffy, but she had a half smile on her face.

"What flavor?" Her voice almost a whisper.

"Surprise me."

Walking away from his sister he fought the urge to look back. It would only make it worse for the both of them. He walked around the corner of the house and right into Jason.

"You ready? Everyone's waiting out front." Jason rubbed his hands together.

"Yeah. Do we have weapons?"

"Got them." He handed Luke an 8-inch blade with a Jade hilt.

Luke ran his finger along the steel.

"Ready to go kick some ugly demon ass?"

Luke hesitated; his friend's tone sounded removed. This was war.

"I'm ready, but are you?"

"Sure, why?"

"Look around, some of us die today. Kicking demon ass sounds like a video game."

Jason peered over his shoulder, most of the group were kids. He closed his eyes and nodded. "You're right. I'm sorry."

Luke cleared his throat, "Let's go."

He leaped, opening his wings and gliding toward the setting sun with Jason on his right and the rest following behind.

Twenty miles was only a few minutes for angels, and they were at their destination before they had time to feel the true exhilaration of flight. The desert sand provided a soft landing, allowing them to move swiftly and silently. The cave was fifty feet away and tucked into the side of a mountain, indigenous terrain of the Mojave Desert—Creosote bush and rabbit brush—provided camouflage to the troop. Ducking low and partially crawling, the plants shielded their movement.

A red glow like fire expelling from a dragon's breath illuminated the mouth of the cave. Luke's heart thumped and his blood roiled when he saw a face he recognized instantly —*Abaddon. How the fuck is this possible?*

Jason leaned in. "How is what possible?"

Luke scowled. "I keep forgetting about the damn angel hearing. See that demon? I left his body on the side of the road in California with a shattered skull."

"Not surprising. You've got to behead them. Especially if they're an arch-demon. Is he?"

"Yup."

"Well, there you go. Kill him with your dagger.

"This ought to be fun. I'm guessing he's pissed off at me."

"I got your back."

The group split in half, flanking the opening like a strategically planned black ops mission. Luke had no idea how many demons were actually in the cave, but he knew Abaddon was not going down easy. He and Jason would take on the arch-demon while the rest of their group made their way into the cave. Once Abaddon was dead, Luke and Jason would join the others. The angels in the other troop would wait for any demons who escaped the cave.

Descending, Luke turned to Jason. "We stay together."

He forced a smile.

Luke sliced through the air and landed about ten feet in front of Abaddon. By the wide eyes and open mouth it was apparent that the demon was surprised to see him. Jason stood beside him with a dagger in his right hand.

Abaddon lunged for Luke who swiftly dodged to his left leaving the arch-demon empty handed. He motioned for the first wave of angels to head into the cave while the others gathered around the opening on either side to catch any demon trying to escape.

Luke flew into the atmosphere with Jason on his heels. They gained speed and dove for Abaddon slamming him into a large boulder and smashing it to pieces. The demon quickly recovered and spread his wings. Reaching for a long blade he had tucked in his belt, he focused on the archangel. With the serrated edge he slashed at Luke, but the teen was too fast. Diving to avoid each attempt as if were a well-choreographed dance, Luke avoided the demons blade.

Jason saw an opportunity and darted down attempting to

thrust the dagger into the demon's back, but the fiend spun around grabbing him by the neck.

Struggling to rip the vise like fingers from his throat, Jason dropped the dagger. Luke plunged toward the earth, catching the blade and rocketing towards his friend. Releasing a wild roar from the pit of his belly, Luke plunged the dagger into the flesh of the demon and gripping with both hands, he ripped Abaddon's head from his body. The demon ignited into a fireball, raining ashes to the ground below.

The friends landed safely and joined the others who were waiting outside the cave.

"Half of you stay here, watch for anyone escaping. The rest come with us."

Only a few demons were present when they got to the enemy's lair. They kept charging the opposition and didn't stop until the last demon servant was lying dead in the ground.

When the battle ended, Luke gazed around the cavern. Three bloody bodies caught his attention. He dropped to his knees and bowed his head over the fallen angels before ordering that they be carried home.

TWELVE

Mary lightly traced the throbbing bruise that was quickly taking shape on her arm. She needed to start turning things around quickly. If Lucifer was coming in three days, that's all the time she had to gain Araqiel's trust. She'd devised and discarded a hundred plans of how to get to Lucifer, but each one ended with failure.

A knock at her bedroom door interrupted her planning. She knew who it was though she always wondered why this demon even bothered knocking. The door locked from the outside, so Mary was a prisoner in her own room. It seemed respect for one's privacy was not a common practice when holding someone against their will. And yet—.

"Come in, Esebelle."

The demon entered with a plate of food in her hand. She was fairly young, or at least she looked young. Maybe no more than thirteen or fourteen, but demons take the form of humans they abducted, so she surmised Esebelle was probably far older. Mary only saw the girl's true, demon face once, right after she arrived. But it wasn't anger that made her reveal her true nature. It was fear; Esebelle feared Araqiel.

"Why do you insist on knocking?"

"You are to be the Dark Princess. I must show respect."

"*The Dark Princess.* I kind of like that."

Mary hated to say the words, but if this wretched thing feared Araqiel, she might want to do something to gain a place in his good graces. *Relaying anything I say to her might do it.*

"Have you ever met our Prince?"

"No. But I hear he is magnificent."

Mary swallowed hard to push back the acid burning her throat. Vomiting in front of this demon was not an option.

"Well, thank you for my food and for knocking."

After Esebelle left, it was clear to Mary what she had to do. Unfortunately, the demon girl's life was about to get horrifying.

She ignored the revolting plate of rare chicken and dry lettuce. She needed to figure out how to make Araqiel think that Esebelle had plotted to kill Lucifer. When she reported the plot to her father, Mary would be assured a place by his side.

It sounded easy enough, but the execution had to be perfect. Sadly, Esebelle would probably wind up dead in the process. But she was a demon and was destined for Hell, which is where Lucifer will wind up. So, it's a win-win for the both of them. Sort of.

Mary and Becca had learned to swap images as a means of communication. They had gotten pretty good at it. She never brought it up to Luke during the entire time they were underground. He was always so concerned about the role she would play in driving the devil back to Hell. If he knew they were speaking on different frequencies, that would only give him more to worry about. Now that Becca could almost see all that Mary did, it definitely aided their plot. Mary needed the dagger with Jesus's hair in the handle and a second one for her plan to work.

She mentally pictured the two daggers. Mary held the authentic blade, and the phony dagger was in the hands of

Esebelle. Concentrating on Becca, the mind connection sent the pictures to her. When an image of both knives and a dead Lucifer appeared in her thoughts, she knew Becca understood what she needed.

Once the demon was out of the picture and Mary had gained Araqiel's confidence, she'd hide the real dagger under her shirt when it came time to meet the devil. She hoped one deep plunge through his heart would be enough because she doubted she'd get a second try.

Mary narrowed her eyes, two more pictures popped into her mind. Becca sent images of angel wings and a clock. Mary knew that meant one of the angels would bring the blades as soon as they could. Now, she waited.

When they arrived home Jason and some of the others took the three bodies of their fallen brothers to the church until the families were notified. Luke immediately sought out Michael and Gabriel to brief them on what had happened.

"Abaddon's dead—for the second time. This one sent him back to hell. We lost three, I'm gonna go talk to their parents."

"Oh son, I'm sorry." Gabriel placed a hand on Luke's back.

"I will tell them." Michael stated.

"No. They're my soldiers, I'll break the news."

Sitting with the first of the three families was the hardest thing he had ever had to do, and it didn't get easier. Each parent he had to tell had the same heartbreaking reaction and it tore up his insides. This was war and he wanted to avoid it with every fiber of his being. The exhilaration he once felt over killing demons quickly turned into sadness and regret. It was a necessity to preserve life on earth but given the choice he would rather find another way.

When he was finished, Luke melted into the couch. He lay

his head back and thought of a brick wall. Behind it, everything bad that had happened. He imagined placing the final layer of bricks and mortar to seal them in. Freeing his mind. The cushion next to him compressed. He opened his eyes to see Becca sitting beside him.

"Mary contacted me."

"Is she okay?"

"Yeah. But she needs help."

Becca explained Mary's plan and the need for the daggers. Luke hung on every word. This was the most he had heard about her since Araqiel abducted her from the tunnel.

"I'll go to her and bring them."

"No. You can't. We'll need you here."

"She's right." His mom and dad walked in with Michael and Uriel.

All of them shook their heads in agreement.

"I know you want to but it's not possible. She has to do something very difficult. You will be a distraction that just might cost lives." His mom squeezed his shoulder. "This time you must sit back."

Damn. She was right. He could get Mary killed.

"If not me, then who?"

"Me," said the familiar voice. Jason stood behind him, his jaw tight and arms folded to his chest.

"What? We'll need you here.

"You'll be fine without me. But I can help Mary get away after she kills Lucifer. Araqiel will be on her heels. We'll lead him right back here. Then we end this thing with him once and for all."

Luke couldn't argue. He hated it, but it made sense. "When do you leave?"

"Now."

"They'll kill you if they catch you."

"That's why I'm not getting caught." Jason flashed a wide grin.

"Hang on a sec." Luke ran into the house and re-emerged a few minutes later. "Give this to Mary for me, okay?" He handed Jason a folded piece of paper.

"You'll see her again."

"Just in case." Luke faintly smiled.

The friends embraced and Jason left. Luke gripped the back of his neck and squeezed. His best friend and the girl he loved were going to be in the same dark place and he had no control.

***

When Becca sent Mary the message that Jason was coming, she shared as much information as she could about the house she was being held in. It was a large ranch style by Lake Mead. Beyond that, Mary wasn't sure. She had glimpsed the front on the outside, her bedroom, and the living room. The rest of the place was off limits. She had a window with bars on it, but Jason would be able to pass the daggers to her. He just needed to find the right window. She tied one sock to a bar, if anyone unlocked the door, she'd have ample time to pull it off.

She peered out of the window hoping to catch sight of him. Becca had said he was there. Mary's stomach rumbled with nerves as she saw someone walking. When he was close enough that she could confirm it was Jason, she pushed her fingers through the bars and wiggled them.

It was so good to see his face beaming back at her.

"Are you okay?"

"Yeah. Better now that I see you. But we need to be fast."

Jason handed her the dagger that contained Jesus's hair first. She quickly took it and placed it under her mattress. Then she took the other blade.

"How's everyone?"

"They're all good. Luke misses you. He wanted me to give you this." Jason handed Mary the note through the bars. Her hands trembled as she unfolded the paper.

Mary, you are my paradise. Forever yours, Luke.

Mary lay her head against the bars and passed the note back to Jason. "I miss him too."

Jason dropped his gaze to the desert sand. "I'll be hiding on the property. When you need me, I'll be ready."

She reached through the bars and Jason touched her fingertips. They exchanged smiles and he disappeared into the fading orange leading into the night sky.

Mary held the image of his face in her mind. It was the closest thing to Luke she could get. Three rapids knocks on the door roiled her stomach, Esebelle was bringing dinner. Mary slipped the dagger into her back pocket before yelling, "Come in. You're right on time tonight. What slop did you bring me now?"

The demon removed the cover to reveal a bloody steak with lumpy mashed potatoes. The juice trickled its way to the mound of white layering them in a gravy of blood. Mary looked away.

"You haven't touched your lunch. You must eat, my Princess. You'll need your strength. Our Prince will arrive sooner than we thought."

"Sooner? What do you mean?"

"He will be here tomorrow."

Mary quivered. She was running out of time. She also needed to let Becca know, but first she had to plant the dagger.

"Esebelle. Would you mind setting my food up over by the window? I'd like to watch the sky while I eat."

"Of course."

The demon sounded genuinely happy that Mary had taken an interest in her food. While her back was turned, Mary slipped the dagger into the thermal bag that she carried the food in.

There were several cloth napkins and Mary buried it at the bottom.

"Oh, this looks nice. Did you make this?"

"No. We have loyal members in town who own a restaurant, they prepare the food and have it delivered daily. However, the cook brought this today, she'll be staying with us in preparation for *His* coming.

"Thank you so much. I really do appreciate everything you do. I'll make sure I tell our Prince exactly how well you treated me."

Esebelle was gushing. Mary hoped that was enough to have her glide out and not think for a second about the bag. When she picked it up, Mary held her breath, but the demon was beaming so brightly it appeared her plan was going to work. Now she just needed to wait a few minutes before summoning Araqiel, ample time to let Becca know what was going on. Instantly, she envisioned a happy face. This was their code for message received.

Mary clenched her fists and banged on the door, yelling for her father. The lock clicked and she stepped back, pinching her cheeks to appear flushed.

"What is going on? They told me you've been screaming for me."

"I think Esebelle is gonna try something. I don't give a shit about Lucifer, but I don't want her to hurt you. You're still my father."

Mary tried desperately not to stray too far from her true character.

"What are talking about? She would never harm me or our Prince. She reveres us both."

"No, she's scared of you. She told me. I thought I saw something in her bag when she took my food out. I didn't want to confront her, but it looked like a large knife."

"And why would she tell you?"

"Because she thinks I'm her Dark Princess. I'm telling you, your demon is delusional."

"We'll see about this."

Araqiel stormed out of the room, locking it. Mary sat at the edge of the bed tapping her leg in anticipation.

She waited for what seemed like hours before she heard the click of the lock opening.

"Please come out and join me in the dining room."

Mary followed Araqiel not knowing if she should be rejoicing or panicking. The table was set for two and he ushered her to the chair on the left side of the head of the table. He pulled the chair out and Mary sat down. Araqiel took his seat. He clapped his hands once and a large robust woman came in holding two white bags. She placed one in front of Mary and then Araqiel.

Turning the bag Mary got a huge grin on her face. The orange Burger Bob's logo and aroma of fresh French fries and a double patty stack made her starving body ignite with glee.

"You got us our burgers. Just like when we first came to Boulder City. I loved that night."

Mary basked in the warmth of happy memories. Crap. She needed to focus. But this was her dad. So few things made her happy growing up, but these souvenirs of their Friday nights together were some of the best times. *But he tried to kill your mother and your boyfriend.* What warm feelings she had quickly dissipated.

"You were right. Esebelle did indeed have a very large knife in her possession. If it weren't for you, I'm not sure how far she would have gotten. Thank you."

"Even with everything that's happened, you know I still love you. You raised me. I wouldn't want anyone to hurt you."

"Well, that's certainly a change from a few days ago."

"I'm not saying I'm signing on for the new world. I'm just

saying, sitting in my room, I've had time to think. I also have been feeling a little weird lately."

"Really? How so?" There was a twinkle of curiosity and excitement in his dark eyes.

Mary knew she had to make this sound good.

"When I was in Boulder City, and I turned, part of me was exhilarated. I've been missing that lately. I don't know how to say it . . . .it made me feel more whole than anything I've done this past year. Things that were important to me when I left seem to be losing their meaning. I can barely remember Lilith's face."

"Important? What things?"

"I used to worry about everyone. Now I feel like they'll be fine doing their own thing. I miss Luke. But I also don't want to be an angel's girlfriend either. It's like there are two of me and one is fighting with the other."

"This is what I've been waiting for. I told you in time you would start to realize your true nature. It's happening."

"No. I'm not choosing this."

"I know it's not what you think you want. But I promise you, if you embrace it, you will be free."

Mary's next move was crucial. One wrong word and they'd be back to where they started.

"What happened to Esebelle?"

"Do you really want to know?"

Mary nodded her head. "Yes."

"First, I ripped off her arms and then her legs. Last was her head. How does that make you feel?"

"Like I'm supposed to feel bad, but I don't. She wanted to kill you and she got what she deserved."

Araqiel didn't utter a word. With a cheeky grin, he took a large bite out of his burger.

Becca ran down the stairs from her bedroom to find Michael. They were all outside training with the younger angels and practicing in flight maneuvers. She yelled up to Michael who quickly plunged towards the earth stopping inches from impact. She told him that Lucifer would be arriving sooner than they'd thought.

When Gabriel and Luke joined him, he filled them in before announcing it to everyone else.

"We need to get word to Jason. He thinks he has a few more days." Luke gasped.

"I've already sent Jeremiah; he's proving to be one of the more skilled of the group. He'll get to Jason. And Becca said Mary's plan has worked. Araqiel thinks she is turning."

"Now we only have to hope that she can do it tomorrow and Jason can get her home."

"I know you're worried, Luke. We will do our part here and they will do theirs."

Michael's words didn't reassure him, but he had no other choice than to wait.

***

Mary couldn't sleep. Her insides vibrated in agony, fear could be paralyzing but this was more like a thousand electrodes attached to every muscle and the dial turned on to maximum capacity. The Dark Prince, an original angel and outcast from heaven, was descending on them tomorrow.

"What the fuck do you do with that?" she whispered to herself. At one point, she got up and strained to look out the window hoping to catch a glimpse of Jason. With pictures of him and Jeremiah flashing in her mind she knew Becca was sending a message. At least he wouldn't be blindsided. After spending much of the night staring up at the ceiling, the darkness finally turned to light. Her bedroom door had been left unlocked. Probably another test. She got up and ambled to the bathroom. It felt good to take a hot shower and wash her hair. Her thoughts wandered to the demon. She must have been so scared. Mary knew it was what she had to do and that Esebelle was, in fact, a demon, but it didn't help to ease her conscience in the least.

After dressing, she went down to breakfast. This was the day everyone in the house had anticipated and they were busy trying to make everything perfect. Even Araqiel was a little distracted. Twice during breakfast Mary had asked him a question, but he didn't respond. Lucifer was due to arrive at noon. Mary had four hours to wait. She had no idea what to expect, only the horrors of all the scary movies she had seen through the years. Satan had been depicted as everything, from a cool and suave handsome man to a creature, eight feet tall with hooves and horns. She preferred the latter. At least with a creature, it wouldn't get confusing.

She decided to take a walk and asked Araqiel if he wanted to accompany her—he did. She hoped it might help melt away some of the doubt he had. What better way to bond than with a one-on-one excursion.

The desert was a peculiar place. It wasn't colorful and yet had an abundance of color—mostly shades of green and brown, but color, nonetheless. Walking away from the house, she gazed over her shoulder and took a long, hard look. Storing to memory anything she might need during her escape later.

Mary kept the conversation light. She reminisced about her childhood in hopes this would soften Araqiel on some level. His short bursts of laughter tickled her ears, the plan just might be working.

"Do you think Lucifer will like me?"

Mary gazed out toward the mountains. Her aspiration was born solely out of deceit. Attempting to sound vulnerable was a ploy to stroke Araqiel's need for superiority.

"Our Prince will love you."

Mary didn't respond. Nor did she ask for him to elaborate. Too much interest would tip him off. There still needed to be some yin and yang when it came to her embracing the darkness.

"I'm getting hungry. How about you?" Mary rubbed her stomach.

"I could eat. I'll have Cook make us some sandwiches."

When they returned to the house, Araqiel instructed the woman to prepare lunch and set the dining room table.

Mary wrinkled her nose as Cook approached with a sandwich and then tried fanning the odor away.

"What is this?"

Cook narrowed her eyes. "Egg salad with relish and onions. It's your father's favorite."

"Oh." Mary swallowed to clear the lump in her throat. "I'm sorry but I don't like eggs. Is there any peanut butter and jelly?"

Araqiel raised a brow. "Mary. Since when don't you eat eggs?"

"Sort of since birth."

"My mistake. I'd forgotten. No worries, Cook will prepare what you requested.

Cook's eyes turned to black and Mary cringed. "That's okay. I can do it myself."

"Nonsense. You stay here with me and she'll have your lunch ready in no time."

Mary wanted to buy more time to soften Araqiel and this certainly did it. She just worried there might be a trace of poison in her sandwich. Never piss off the cook.

With each moment she spent with Araqiel her head ached. Hating him for all the lies and what his true nature was directly conflicted with her yearning to have the kind of father she wanted in her life. Darkness crept into her heart, and she needed to concentrate on the warmth of the light—imagine it flowing through her, filling every crevice. She focused her thoughts on the task of literally saving the world and everyone she loved. She allowed her mind to take her away until she was abruptly interrupted by one of the demon henchmen barging through the door dragging a half-conscious Jason behind him. Mary's heart stopped.

"Shall I kill him?" His fists were now firmly wrapped around Jason's neck.

Araqiel wiped the corners of his mouth with a napkin and then got up.

"Well, what do we have here? A wayward angel coming to save my daughter, no doubt."

Mary wanted to obliterate the demon and her father, but she knew the wrong move now would ruin the progress she had made.

"Let's find out. Let him go." Mary's voice embraced the dark within her.

The demon hesitated.

"I said, LET HIM GO!"

The demon released his hold and Jason fell to the floor. Araqiel smirked with delight. His daughter's face reflected the command in her voice.

"I'd leave if I were you." Araqiel waved his hand toward the door. "She is not happy."

The demon lowered his head before exiting.

Jason was still holding his neck as he glanced at the watch on his wrist and then to the two pieces of black coal that filled Mary's eyes. She gave him a slight tilt of the head hoping he understood she got the reference. It was almost time.

Flashes zapped in her brain so suddenly it made the room spin. The salt was pungent on her lips—she was sweating. Becca was trying to communicate. Mary tried to cough her body back into control, but it didn't work. The images were coming too quickly. She couldn't sort through the barrage that was penetrating her brain and pushing through to her flesh. She grabbed her forehead and pressed into it with the palm of her hand trying to suppress the pain.

"Mary what's wrong? You're dripping with sweat." Araqiel pursed his lips while studying her movement.

"I'm fine. I think I need to go and put water on my face. It could just be exhaustion. It's been a rough few days. Hold him until I get back, would you? I'd like the pleasure if you don't mind."

"Of course. But be quick."

"I will."

Once in her room she took the dagger out from under the mattress. Removing the lock of Jesus' hair from the protective pouch, she placed it into the hidden compartment of the blade's handle and tucked it in the pocket of her hoodie. She also made sure she had the small pocketknife she normally kept with her wherever she went—something her dad made her do. It really made no sense. She could snap a person in two with her thoughts. But something told her to take it and she listened to her instinct.

The pictures Becca was sending became clear. Jason will be in the room when Lucifer arrives in case she needs help. Mary jolted when she heard the loud gong coming from outside the house. He was here.

Touching the knob, her hand smeared off the brass like butter melting off toast. She rubbed them along the sleeves of her hoodie before grabbing it again. The hallway to the living room felt more like the path to the gas chamber. Death would be easier than what was coming for her. How could she fool the devil?

The angels were lined up in a strategic position on Ramona Lane. Lining the block on both sides would force the demons to come down the center where they could surround them. The pain jabbing in Luke's chest was a constant reminder of what they were about to do. Josiah had taken a place next to him in the line. He didn't want to be distracted by worrying about the kids' safety, but no time for arguments.

A cloud of dust rushed down the center of the street creating a dark mass of sand and debris twirling its way into a funnel.

"Josiah, get ready. They're here."

The boy nodded and moved closer to Luke.

Lilith was across the street with Samael and several archangels who surrounded the younger, less experienced ones.

A thick, dense cloud of dust stole their clear vision. Luke tried to rise above it, but something held him back. He struggled to gain control as two large demons had him in their grips. One relentlessly pushed down his wings while the other attempted to hold them. He spun his body into a backflip coming up with a punch to the jaw and then a kick to others chest. They were catapulted from sight.

Luke reached for Josiah, but the boy was gone. Straining to see beyond the wall of sand, he was taken by surprise with a blow from behind that tossed him directly into the spinning cloud of debris. Grains of sand cut his flesh like shards of glass and he raised his arms up trying to shield his eyes. Barely able to see, he blindly forced his way through the chaos. Demons and angels were in hand-to-hand combat all around him. His wings extended, only to be shoved down by the weight of the wind. Someone grabbed the back of his neck and Luke found himself defending his life alongside his brothers.

The demon had a firm grip around his throat and Luke kicked furiously to wriggle free. With the strength of ten men, his neck bulged under the steel grip of his opponent. His heart slowed with every denial of breath and Luke could no longer gain control of his arms and legs. Leaving his shell, he floated above to see the full view of the warrior that was about to end his life. Pointing his hands toward the demon, the rays of light struck the monstrosity by surprise, and it instinctively loosened its grip to shield its eyes.

Like a bullet leaving the chamber, Luke's spirit slammed into his body and swiftly removed the dagger he had in a sheath on his belt. Stepping behind the demon, he penetrated his flesh until he could feel the blood flow through his fingers. Then pushing the knife clear to the back of his neck, he sawed the demon's head off. The body thudded as it hit the asphalt, its head rolling into the curb. Luke wiped his hands on the sides of his jeans as he searched for his next victory. Half-way down the block, Lilith was surrounded by three pus-ridden creatures who were winning the battle. Pushing against the wind, his legs felt like he was stepping through cement. This time he wouldn't be surprised. This time, he was the one who would attack.

When he reached them, Lilith was in the throes of fighting two of the beasts at the same time while the third watched with ear piercing laughter. He was the first to go. Luke pounced on top of him and with both hands took a firm grip on his head and twisted until he heard the snapping of bones and the creature's limp body fell to the ground. Charging toward the remaining two, Luke pressed a firm grip onto the shoulder of the larger beast, ripping it from Lilith. Side by side they fought until both creatures were dead.

"You okay?" Luke asked Lilith.

"Yeah. You?"

"I'm good. But I lost track of Josiah."

Lilith was about to answer, but she was side swiped and fell hard onto the ground. Luke reached for her, but Samael interjected.

"I got this." Samael lifted her up and set her to the side of the street before rejoining the battle.

Luke's adrenaline was food for his angel half. He no longer struggled through the whipping wind. Walking with ease, he grabbed demon after demon and slaughtered them. Slicing throats, ripping limbs off, and splitting them like a wishbone—each kill grew more gruesome. He stopped when he realized the streets were almost void of battle. The remaining angels had full control of the grounds and the air began to settle.

Eyes drawn to the heavens and the battle above, he cut through the sky to join Michael, Gabriel, and several other archangels, who had overtaken the last wave. Golden rays replaced the darkness but couldn't warm the horror that Luke felt from the picture below. Bloody and broken bodies carpeted the once serene Ramona Lane. Acid rose and pooled in the back of his throat sending a ripple of nausea that consumed his gut. Images of wrenching limbs and tearing flesh ate through his mind, stealing away his reason for battle.

Touching pavement, he looked about himself, the view from the ground was much worse. Luke was standing in the middle of an apocalyptic graveyard with bodies piled up that were reminiscent of World War II death camps. Only they were not all innocent humans. Many of them were soldiers from Hell that were sent to destroy everything he loved. It was the others that left a void inside. His fallen brothers. Sensing someone near him, he turned to see Josiah standing beside him. Tears were streaming down the young angel's face. Extending out his arms, Luke encompassed the boy in a tight hug.

Mary tried to calm the pounding in her chest. Closing her eyes, she focused on Luke, it soothed her enough to keep going. She reached the end of the hall and rounded the corner into the living room.

The visitor stood at the window with his back to them. He wasn't very tall, maybe five feet eight or nine, his blonde hair neatly trimmed like the heartthrob from a '90's boy band. He had a slender build and wore faded jeans with a dark blue dress shirt casually untucked. His hands were clasped behind his back. Araqiel was sitting on the couch and there were two very large men dressed all in black towering over the visitor on either side. Jason was in a wooden chair with his hands and feet bound by duct tape. Her eyes immediately met his and sweat beaded up across her forehead. She took a seat next to her father.

Pictures of the front of the house and the grounds, along with the room, and their visitor, filled her mind and floated away bringing news of the meeting to Becca.

Mary received the message of the terrifying battle taking place on Ramona Lane. The block littered with carnage of demons and angels alike came upon her with consternate suddenness and she stiffened her back to gain control over her trembling body. The next few minutes meant life or death to her, Jason, and the world.

"My Prince, allow me to introduce you to my daughter, Mary."

Araqiel made the words drip from his lips like he was savoring a decadent dessert. His voice smooth and melodic. Mary shuddered. The stranger turned around and stole her gaze. Honey bangs fringed across his forehead softening the penetrating glare of his powder blue eyes. Under other circumstances, Mary would've thought the stranger handsome, but she knew better. This shell belonged to some unlucky bastard whose life had been stolen in the name of the Dark Prince. She knew the truth behind the beauty—a soul as black as coal.

"Your father tells me wonderful things about you, but none of which come close to the immense beauty you are. My girl, you are ravishing. The spitting image of your mother. Please stand up. I want to take in all of you."

Mary could barely keep it together as the visitor took in an obnoxious breath and released it while holding his hand over his heart.

"Just sensational. However, I do sense some hesitation. Your body betrays you. Maybe it's because we haven't been properly introduced. Allow me . . . I am Lucifer." He clasped her hand and turned it to the fleshy underside. Kissing gently along her wrist and forearm, he hesitated and then licked her fingers. "I am Lord of Hell and soon—the world." Lucifer leered.

Mary swallowed back the remnants of cheeseburger and fries trying to come up. "Not hesitant, my Prince. Although it's true that I didn't see things clearly in the beginning. But the past few days with my father have helped me embrace the true darkness within me. I no longer care to hide who I am."

Lucifer closed what little space was left between them before closing his eyes and breathing in her scent. The two guards positioned themselves beside him and in front of Mary. She clenched her jaw and bit the inside of her cheek.

"And who are you?" Lucifer licked his lips.

"Mary. Daughter of the archdemon Araqiel and Lilith, the most powerful woman to be born. I am the darkness and cunning of my father with the beauty of my mother. The world is too simple to understand my power." Mary bit her lip.

"I'm tingling in my loins. Araqiel, you didn't tell me how utterly scrumptious she is."

"Mary, no. You can't. Don't give in." Jason pleaded.

Mary swiftly spun around and in seconds her eyes had darkened, and the once beautiful face had turned into the demon she harbored inside.

"Shut up." Mary bellowed.

"Mary, this isn't you." Jason wriggled to break the tape.

Mary knew what she had to do. With two strides, she was on top of him and her face inches from his. She locked eyes and stared for a moment hoping he would trust in what she was about to do. Firmly she clasped both hands around his throat and squeezed. His face contorted as he struggled to fight back but the constraints were too tight. When he passed out, she stepped back. She knew if she was going to win over Lucifer, her behavior must make a statement. Fortunately, Mary could hear Jason's heart as clearly as if it were beating in her own chest. She could only assume she had procured super hearing. It came without warning, but she welcomed it. Hoping her father and the ruler of Hell were too occupied with self-love to notice the faint thumping of Jason's life force, she quickly spun around to face them and grinned.

She held onto the demon face this time. Normally it would change back without her having any control, but today was different. It was at her command. Hmm. Another procurement. Mary faced Lucifer with vacant black eyes. He smiled and caressed her cheek. Holding back the disdain she felt, she prayed the small pocketknife she'd slipped into Jason's right hand wouldn't fall to the floor when he woke up.

"This is your true nature, my Princess. I am so pleased. Araqiel, you have done stupendously."

Lucifer snapped his fingers and ordered the guards to leave. Mary swayed as the blood raced to her head. She would be alone with the Prince of Darkness with only one thing in her way— her father. The two goons hesitated, but quickly obeyed with one glare from Lucifer.

"Now Mary, my love, let's discuss our future. We will have many children and they will populate this world with hate, darkness, and every vice known to man. If you would like, some of your favorite humans can be kept as our slaves. But the rest I will send back to my father. He can have his precious species, after a few years of torture of course. They will beg for death, and he will do nothing as he always does. The world will be a beautiful wickedness where I will finally be free. I've been in the confines of Hell for entirely too many years.

"As for my former home. I think it's time my brothers take

residence there. They cast me out so easily. Turning their backs and never once trying to see my side. They will suffer like I have. Hell will be their reward for abandoning me."

Mary moved closer to Lucifer with her hand in the front pocket of her hoodie and firmly gripping the dagger.

Rubbing her upper torso against his back, she slowly leaned in and subtly kissed the nape of his neck. Lucifer moaned with ecstasy and pressed into her chest. Mary gaped at Araqiel. His eyes were wide with delight. Her body was doing the job she needed it to, but her mind was exploding with anger. Her Father's evil was now completely revealed. Any normal father would try to save his daughter. Araqiel was basking in the pleasure.

"Ohhhh." Jason moaned.

Mary's left hand crept around Lucifer's side to his chest. The devil was so enthralled with her he paid no attention to the waking Jason. She peeked again at Araqiel through the locks of hair that had fallen in front of her face. His eyes never left them.

Unbuttoning Lucifer's shirt one at a time to keep him distracted, her right hand grabbed the handle of the dagger with a firm grip. Moving in front of him she leaned in and caressed his chest with her lips. He reached under her chin and gazed into her eyes. For a moment Mary saw his true face. Horribly disfigured with thick horns protruding from the top of a largely sloping forehead, she didn't look away. He pressed his lips to hers as she pulled out the dagger, plunged it into his heart and twisted it.

Lucifer slowly lifted his head, his eyes wide in disbelief. Traveling his gaze from Mary to the handle of the blade, he grasped it with both hands and yanked the dagger from his chest. Reaching out for her, she instinctively backed away. He stumbled, and grabbing the back of the leather chair, tried to cling on while his hands slid down, leaving a trail of human blood. Mary watched as he gradually slithered down the chair and onto the floor. Gurgling, he struggled to lift his head before convulsing and then igniting into flames.

"Nooooo!" Araqiel ran to the charred remains and then set his sights on his daughter. His body doubled in size, his distorted face oozed with pus from open sores and his coal, black eyes reflected death to his once child of hope. He lunged toward her but not before Jason broke free and slammed him into the wall. Hearing the commotion, the two guards rushed in, nostrils flaring.

Mary called her inner demon and with one flick of her wrist the two crashed through the window, shattering the glass and landing on top of the SUV in the driveway. She grabbed Jason's hand and they jumped out of the window and ran. Jason's wings unfolded and he took a firm grip around Mary's arm, but something stopped him from lifting off. She was instantly pulled back and fell to the ground. Dazed, she tried to get up, but her balance was off and plop—she was back on the ground.

"Mary! Fulfillment!" Jason pointed behind her.

Mary turned to see the most beautiful jet-black wings draping around her. She stood up and concentrated on moving them. In moments, they were flapping, and she was hovering above the ground. Her enhanced hearing was detecting a third heartbeat and she wasn't waiting to find out who it was. She followed Jason into the clouds and back to Ramona Lane.

When they reached Luke's house, everyone was waiting for them. Mary scanned the faces for the one she could not wait another minute to see. He was standing against the wall with Becca and Lilith beside him. Luke turned and ran to her, holding Mary by the waist, he pulled her close. Leaning in, he brushed his lips across hers before passionately lingering.

When they parted, Mary hugged Lilith and Becca. "Lucifer's gone. But before we left, I heard another heartbeat."

"What do you mean you heard a heartbeat?" Luke asked.

"I can hear things that I couldn't before. It's like super hearing." Mary grinned.

"Wings, super hearing and a demon self. Remind me not to piss you off. It was probably Araqiel. We've been waiting for him."

"Look what I found." Josiah held out his hand.

"What do you have?" Luke took a silver locket from his hands.

Mary froze. "Where did you get that?" Her voice trembled.

"Do you know what it is?" Luke questioned.

"My father gave that to me when I was a little girl. It had a picture of me and him in it."

Luke opened the locket. A much younger Araqiel held a baby girl.

"Where was this?"

"It was on the . . ." Josiah's eyes fluttered. He coughed as blood trickled from his mouth. He collapsed to the ground.

"Josiah!" Luke and Mary dropped down next to him, cradling the boy in their arms. An arrow protruded from the middle of his back. Luke jumped up, circling the trees, he spotted Araqiel.

"How could you? He's a child!" Mary screamed.

Mary took hold of the darkness letting it spill out to every inch of her now erect body. Luke's eyes widened as his love embraced the transformation, the light extinguished by a single act of evil. The vivid white clouds peeled away to reveal ink black, flowing masses of shields to the electric storm brewing behind them. The skies crackled and the heavens opened raining blood of terror on the ground below.

"Mary. No!"

Luke yelled in vain. Mary's sites were glued to Araqiel, and she would not be deterred.

"He has to die. For Josiah, for all the slain children he was responsible for and their families. For me and my mother and for all the evil he wraps around his demon body like a warm blanket. He deserves a slow death, one cultivated over centuries. Piece by piece by piece."

Luke gasped. He needed to act quickly, or he'd lose her to the darkness forever. He furiously searched for Lilith and spotted her just as she was running to her daughter. He stepped in front of her and intervened. Pulling her to the sidewalk.

"Let me go. Can't you see what's happening. She's lost control. I have to stop her." Lilith pushed away from Luke.

"She's not gonna stop until Araqiel's dead. And she can't be the one to do it."

"Yes. We'll surely lose her to hell if she does," said Lilith. "What do you propose?"

"Keep her occupied for just a second, long enough for me to reach Araqiel. I'll do the rest. He needs to die at my hand not hers."

Lilith moved slowly toward her daughter, coming up from behind. She caught the attention of Samael and nodded for him to join her. He moved into position on the other side of Mary and waited.

"Now!" Luke shouted.

Both Lilith and Samael reached out tightening their arms around Mary's body, but they were no match for her newfound hate. With the turn of a finger they were both thrust backwards, their bodies dragging along the black top.

Watching the menagerie of errors unfold, Araqiel didn't utter a word. He just flashed a maniacal grin as he dove in front of Mary and plunged a dagger into her stomach. Mary's body crumbled to the red stained asphalt.

"Mary!" Luke knelt down beside her and lifted her into his arms.

"I . . . I'm." Mary's head dropped back.

Lilith ran to her daughter and took her from Luke.

Clenching his fists, Luke let anger guide him. His soul

burned for revenge. Like a missile he shot straight for his intended target. He was so fast Araqiel didn't have time to move out of the way and Luke hit him with every ounce of vindication his soul could convey. The two men were thrown, spinning uncontrollably through the clouds. Luke relaxed his body and let the ride take him. He knew if he fought it, the spinning would just get worse. Slowly he gained control and was able to halt moments before he hit the asphalt. Araqiel wasn't as lucky. The impact sent a resounding roar as the earth beneath cracked from the impact. Landing beside the unconscious arch-demon, Luke acted impulsively. Reaching for the dagger on his hip, he pierced Araqiel's throat, driving the blade into the neck and sawing his flesh and bone until the demon's head hung from his grip.

Hands bloodied he dropped the blade on the ground and collapsed.

Rushing to their son's side, Gabriel and Cassie picked him up and brought him to his bedroom. Placing him on his bed, Cassie sat by his side . . . waiting.

It was hours before Luke woke up. Slowly opening his eyes, he saw the remnants of dried blood on his knuckles—everything came back to him. He turned to his side and like a river the emotions gushed through his shaking body.

Cassie tried to soothe her son. "It'll get better, I promise."

"Mom, I . . ."

Before he could finish his thoughts, the door creaked open, and he heard the most beautiful sound. "Hey. You awake?"

Luke abruptly turned to the door. "Mary?"

Cassie stood. "I'll leave you two but when you're ready, come downstairs and eat something. You need to regain your strength."

"I will."

Luke scrambled out of bed and wrapped Mary in a tight embrace. He was afraid it was just a dream; afraid she was still lost to him forever.

Nuzzling close to her ear, he whispered, "I thought you were dead. The pain..."

"Shhh, it's okay. I'm here and I'm not going anywhere. Lilith brought me to Rita. I felt my spirit going but Rita pulled it back just in time."

"Josiah?"

Mary shook her head no. "It was too late. Rita couldn't save him, he died instantly."

Tears pooled in Lukes eyes. "I thought we lost you to the darkness. I was so scared."

"I know, I thought I'd lost myself. The power, it was unlike anything I could've imagined. It frightened me beyond words and yet felt comforting at the same time. I'm still scared. Scared I'll turn one day and hurt you or someone else I love."

"It won't happen."

"How can you be so sure? You saw what I was, what I became."

"Because like today, I'll be by your side. Your personal little archangel ready to slay evil whenever it tries to take you."

Mary didn't utter a word. She knew his words were true, but she'd be powerless if she let go of her humanity. A black stain singed into her soul would forever mark her and given the right circumstances she wasn't as sure as Luke about her ability to stay in the light.

"How are you? Do you think you can walk?" Mary kissed his cheek.

"I think I'm okay." He smiled.

"Your dad is downstairs waiting for you. Everyone else has gone home." She caressed the hair away from his forehead.

"And Michael?"

"He's gone, too. All the archangels have left. It's over."

Luke hobbled to his bed and threw the blanket around him. He wanted to see his dad. He needed to see him. Mary helped him downstairs and into the kitchen. She knew they needed some time, so she decided to seek solace by the pool.

His father was eating a sandwich while his mom poured a glass of wine.

"Mom. Dad." He sat down at the table.

"How are you feeling?"

"Like a train hit me." He slumped in the chair.

"It'll pass in a few days. You just need to rest and get some food into your body." Gabriel grinned. "It's done. Mary saved humanity from Lucifer, and we won our war."

"But what's gonna happen to Lucifer's followers?"

"There are those who will always be loyal to Satan. But we will stop them if they try to rise up."

Luke peered out the glass doors to the backyard. Just a few hours ago the scene was very different and the outcome unclear. So much had changed in the past year, life would never be simple again. A dust of light twinkled across the blades of grass like fairy's enjoying the day. He caught a glimpse of Mary as she snuggled in one of the patio chairs, a dampened smile reflecting back at him from the glass. Life would never be the same on Ramona Lane again.

COMING SOON

Liminal Space
July 2024

Acknowledgments

For my friends who are here and those who are not, thank you for always listening to my rants about my writing career and for reading every piece of work I've ever written...even the bad stuff.

Quote:

There is nothing to writing.

All you do is sit down at a typewriter and bleed.

~Ernest Hemingway

About the Author

Originally from New York, Vicki-Ann is an award-winning author and short screenplay writer. She currently resides in Nevada. Writing Young Adult paranormal, she finds inspiration from events that have been in her life for as long as she can remember. Inheriting the sensitivity to the supernatural from her family, they continue to be an endless source of vision.